Jane awoke to the sensation of a warm, heavy body pressed up against hers.

Opening her eyes, she found herself gazing into another pair of eyes, full of soulful adoration.

'Hello,' she said, scratching her companion's enormous ears. 'I thought you were sleeping outside?' Perry sighed and snuggled closer. 'You're not going to make a habit of this. You're lovely, but you're not the one I want to cuddle. Off with you!'

She pulled a cotton dressing gown on and stepped outside. The sun was just up, the dew was still on the ground. And there, wearing only his pyjama trousers, barefoot in the grass, was her beloved. Jane watched fondly as Gil threw up his arms to the sky as if embracing the whole world.

Perry bounded over, barking excitedly.

Lucy Gordon cut her writing teeth on magazine journalism, interviewing many of the world's most interesting men, including Warren Beatty, Richard Chamberlain, Roger Moore, Sir Alec Guinness and Sir John Gielgud. She has also camped out with lions in Africa, and has had many other unusual experiences which have often provided the background for her books. She is married to a Venetian, whom she met while on holiday in Venice. They got engaged within two days and have now been married for twenty-five years. They live in the Midlands, with their three dogs.

One of her books, SONG OF THE LORELEI, won the Romance Writers of America RITA award in 1990, in the Best Traditional Romance category.

Recent titles by the same author:

FOR THE LOVE OF EMMA

REBEL IN DISGUISE

BY
LUCY GORDON

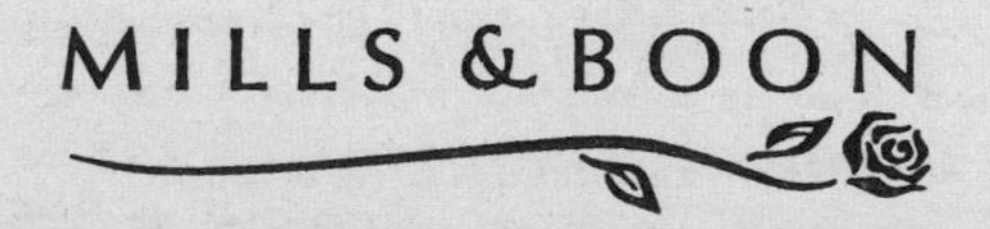

Harlequin Mills & Boon Limited,
Eton House, 18-24 Paradise Road, Richmond, Surrey TW9 1SR

ISBN 0 263 79818 6

Set in Times Roman 10 on 12 pt.
02-9611-52360 C1

Made and printed in Great Britain

CHAPTER ONE

AFTER six months Jane still knew a moment of delight as she entered the bank and saw the plaque on her office door: 'Jane Landers, Manager.'

Of course, this was the smaller of the two branches of Kells Bank in Wellhampton, and Wellhampton itself was only a small market town, although a very prosperous one. But at twenty-six she was the youngest branch manager in Kells, and marked for higher things.

She walked in, a slender, erect figure with fair hair cropped boyishly short, wearing an elegant, charcoal-grey business suit with white lapels. She'd dressed with slightly more formality than usual today because this afternoon she had a meeting with her senior staff, and one or two of them would try to catch her out. They'd had their own preferred candidate for her job, and were inclined to be dismissive of a woman who was not only young but also committed the extra crime of being beautiful in a classical, slightly austere style.

In the early weeks Jane had had to impose her will with a cool firmness that had come as a nasty shock to some of them. She had less trouble now, but she needed to keep on her toes. Her secret weapon was a pair of glasses with severe black rims. In fact her eyesight was perfect and the frames contained only plain glass. She slipped them on when she wished to appear formidable.

As she made her way across the marble floor to her door she glanced at the small group of people waiting to see her. First in line was a young man who looked so wildly out of place in these sedate surroundings that Jane almost stared. He wore black leather trousers with metal studs along the pockets, and a black, skin-tight T-shirt that revealed every line of a lean, muscular torso. His dark, wavy hair touched his collar, and a hint of stubble on his chin and his upper lip threw his curved, firm-lipped mouth into vivid relief. He might have been a bandit, ready to throw a maiden across his saddle and carry her deep into mountainous regions—or a pirate, abducting her in his galleon.

Jane shook her head, wondering where such absurd thoughts had come from. She wasn't normally a fanciful person. But there was something about the young man that made the air tingle. She forced herself back to reality.

Next to him was a large, middle-aged man called John Bridge, who kept looking at his watch and tutting. After that, to Jane's dismay, was Mrs Callam, an elderly widow who lived on a fixed income that was worth less by the day. She came from another age, had no understanding of how money worked, but possessed a touching faith that Jane could make all her problems vanish.

Things were evidently worse than usual today because Mrs Callam jumped up to grasp her arm and began to pour out her story. At once Mr Bridge snapped, 'There is a queue, you know.'

'Oh, dear,' Mrs Callam gasped. 'I'm so sorry, but you see—'

'I detest queue-jumpers.' Mr Bridge had a loud, ugly voice and a surly manner calculated to set people against him even when he was technically in the right.

'I don't see any queue-jumpers,' observed the pirate mildly.

'Nonsense. You saw this woman push her way to the head of the queue.'

'She didn't push her way,' the young man said. 'I was at the head of the queue and I offered to exchange places with her. Like that, see?' He rose and went to the seat on the other side of John Bridge, which Mrs Callam had just vacated. 'Now she's got my place, I've got hers, and you're still second, where you were before. No need to make a fuss about it.' He smiled kindly at Mrs Callam. 'Everything's fine.'

'Oh, thank you, thank you,' she said tearfully. She clutched Jane's arm harder and began to babble, 'So sorry—didn't mean to overdraw and when I saw the charges—' She was almost in tears.

'We do have to make a referral charge when a payment is queried,' Jane said gently, 'but for a long-standing and valued customer like yourself— Harry, could you come here a moment?'

A young man with a kind, plain face came out from behind his counter. 'Mrs Callam accidentally went into overdraft,' Jane told him. 'We'll waive the charges. Harry will sort it out for you, Mrs Callam.'

'Oh, thank you—' She went off with Harry.

Jane turned and found the pirate looking at her with a faint smile. It didn't just touch his lips but also his eyes, which were the darkest blue she'd ever seen. She was conscious of an overpowering impulse to smile back at him.

'Am I going to be kept waiting much longer?' John Bridge demanded.

'Please come in now, Mr Bridge,' Jane said coolly. 'Although, as I explained in my letter, there's really nothing that I can do for you.'

There followed a tough fifteen minutes during which John Bridge tried to coerce her into extending an overdraft that had grown unmanageable through his own folly. His failure left him furious and ill-mannered.

'I'll be writing to head office about you,' he stormed as Jane ushered him out.

'That might be your best plan,' she agreed coolly. 'Good day, Mr Bridge.' She smiled at the pirate. 'I'll be with you in a moment.'

'No rush,' he told her amiably. 'I'm happy as I am.' He indicated Mrs Callam who'd reappeared and was sitting beside him, looking much more cheerful.

She closed her office door, but could still hear John Bridge saying, 'You needn't think you'll get anywhere with the Iron Maiden in there.'

'Maybe not,' came the young man's reply. 'But then I wasn't blessed with your charm and sophistication.'

Jane's lips twitched. Whatever he was doing in the bank he certainly brightened the place up.

Before allowing him in she put through a call in response to a note her secretary had left on her desk. 'Mr Grant, please,' she said. 'Kenneth? I got your message.'

Kenneth Grant was a local businessman she'd been dating recently. He was upright, respectable, a pillar of the community, and in every way suitable for the youngest manager of Kells. His voice was warm when he heard her.

'Just checking that we're still on for tonight,' he said. 'I've booked a table at your favourite restaurant.'

'Mm, looking forward to it.'

'I'll pick you up at seven.'

'I'll be ready on the dot.'

'I know you will. That's one of the nicest things about you, darling. You never keep me waiting.'

She chuckled. 'I hope that's a joke.'

'Of course it's not. You're always punctual.'

'Yes, but—what I meant—' She gave up. She was fond of Kenneth but he could be heavy going. It wouldn't occur to him that to praise a lady's punctuality wasn't the fastest way to her heart. Smiling wryly, she replaced the receiver.

She opened her door and smiled at the young man. 'You can come in now.'

Mrs Callam laid a hand on his arm. 'You've been so kind.'

'It was my pleasure, sweetheart,' he said, smiling at her and putting his hand over hers. He had a brilliant smile, warm and full of charm, and it lit up his surroundings.

He rose, revealing himself as long and lean. In Jane's office he settled himself into the chair facing her desk and stretched out his long legs, seeking a comfortable position. He looked incongruous in the demure office, less because of his clothes than because of the anarchic gleam in his eyes. It was the gleam that caught Jane's attention and made her say disapprovingly, 'That was an outrageous thing you just said.'

'What? What did I say?' He looked innocence personified.

'Calling Mrs Callam sweetheart. She's old enough to be your grandmother, and deserves some respect.'

'Did I offend her? She didn't seem offended.'

'That's not the—'

'Did *you* think she was offended?'

Jane was about to reply severely when her sense of justice intervened. Mrs Callam hadn't been offended. She'd been charmed.

'It's a question of context,' he mused. 'Now if the other fellow had called her sweetheart that would have been an insult.'

Reluctantly Jane realised that he was right. His words had been made against a background of kindness that robbed them of any offence.

'I didn't like your ill-favoured friend,' he observed.

'He's no friend of mine,' Jane couldn't resist saying. 'I think he's one of the most unpleasant bullies I've ever met.'

'Meaning he tried to bully you? But he didn't get anywhere.'

'Since he called me the Iron Maiden you can assume that he didn't.'

He grinned and it was as though a light had come on inside him. The office glowed.

He had a fascinating face, she realised. If its individual features had been regular it would have been more handsome but less interesting. The high forehead and long nose might have belonged to a professor. The laughing eyes and mobile mouth suggested a clown, and somewhere in the firmly outlined chin lurked the stubbornness of a mule. He was a mass of contrasts, and Jane, whose life was governed by the precision of figures, felt an alarming disturbance somewhere within her, as though his company was a delight.

'I'll bet you're not scared of bullying,' he said, as though she'd confirmed some previously held opinion of her.

This would never do. She must get back in control of the conversation. Assuming her severest manner, she said, 'No, I'm not scared of bullying. Neither am I moved by charm.'

'Charm?' He stared as if she'd used a word he'd never encountered before. 'Charm. You mean *me*? Well, I'm flattered, of course, but—'

'What I think,' she said, gathering her fractured dignity about her, 'is that it's time you told me what you want.'

'Two thousand pounds, please.'

She smiled. 'Don't we all? Now, be serious. Why have you come to see me?'

'But I've just told you. I want a loan of two thousand pounds. Why are you surprised? I can't be the first man who's come in here asking for money.'

'Yes, but most of them—' She checked herself. Usually she was as good at guarding her tongue as a bank manager needed to be, but something about this man affected her oddly, making discretion seem like an eccentricity.

'Most of them don't look like one of Hell's Angels,' he finished for her amiably.

'Since you put it like that, yes.'

'Isn't it rather dangerous to judge by appearances?'

'I'm not—precisely—doing that.'

'But that is precisely what you are doing. When I first mentioned a loan, you assumed it was a joke. Why? Because of my appearance.'

Jane drew a paper towards her. 'Suppose we start with some details. May I have your name?'

'Gil Wakeham.'

'Gil—short for Gilbert?'

He made a face. 'I dislike Gilbert. He's a stuffed shirt.'

'I'd be surprised to learn that Gil so much as owns a shirt,' she said wryly.

'I did have a shirt,' he said defensively. 'Once.'

'What happened?' she couldn't resist asking.

'I put it into the wrong wash at the launderette and it came out like a rainbow.'

'I can believe that,' she informed him.

'Since then I've tended to stick to black. It's safer. But I could buy another shirt, if you like.'

'I don't think that would help matters.'

'Oh.' He considered. 'I've got a tie—somewhere.'

Jane fought for control but the deceptive innocence in his eyes was too much for her. Her mouth insisted on smiling and the next moment she was laughing out loud. He laughed with her. 'That's better,' he said. 'I won.'

'Won what?'

'I had a bet with myself that I'd make you laugh in less than five minutes. You should laugh more. It makes you beautiful. It's the real you.'

'You know nothing about the real me,' she said, imposing order on herself at last. 'And if you want any hope of a loan you'd better start behaving like a respectable client.' A teasing imp, who'd never troubled her before, impelled her to add, 'If you know how.'

'I don't,' he said at once. 'But you could instruct me. How should I act? Like the yob who was in here before me?'

'Like a sober, sensible man,' she advised him.

'Is that the kind of man you like? Sober and sensible?'

'It's the kind who gets loans.'

He regarded her, his head on one side. 'But that's not what I asked. What kind of man do you like?'

She put her pen down. 'Mr Wakeham, little though you seem to appreciate the fact, I am a bank manager. And the kind of man I like to see facing me across this desk has a sense of responsibility and doesn't waste my time.'

'And what kind of man do you like to see facing you across a dinner table?'

'One who's wearing a tie,' she said, speaking as severely as possible because she was unnerved by her inability to restrain him.

'I suppose your boyfriend wears a tie,' he said.

'I refuse to discuss this matter with you.'

Gil didn't seem to notice that he'd been snubbed. 'He's probably got more than one tie, as well. Not like me.'

'I don't think I know *anyone* like you,' she said, exasperated.

'And he's upright, serious-minded, and admires you for your sterling qualities.'

Coming so soon after Kenneth's admiration of her punctuality, this remark touched a raw nerve. The conversation had gone quite far enough. Firmly Jane took out her 'formidable' glasses and put them on.

'Perhaps I can take some details,' she said in a voice designed to be quelling. 'Your name is Gilbert Wakeham. Your date of birth?'

He gave it, revealing himself as thirty-five years old. Jane looked at him quickly.

'Yes,' he said, accurately reading her expression. 'I'm not the callow youth that you thought.'

'You're certainly older than you appear.' But now she looked more closely she could see that he did indeed have the face of a man in his mid-thirties. It was his lean frame and light-hearted manner that had fooled her.

'Your address?' she asked.

She thought he hesitated for a moment before saying, 'I have a caravan.'

Jane set down her pen again with a sigh. 'You can't seriously have thought I'd give a loan to a man with no fixed abode?'

'I did before you put those glasses on.'

'I have a lot of people to see.'

'But I haven't told you about my business yet. Here.' He produced a photo album and opened it on the desk before her. It was full of large photographs of fireworks exploding in dazzling colours: pinks, blues, reds, greens, yellows and glittering white. Sometimes they fell like showers of gorgeous rain. Sometimes they were set pieces that shimmered against the black sky.

'This is my business,' he said. 'I hire myself out to give firework displays whenever I'm needed, all over the country. A caravan is simply the most efficient way of living and working.'

'Why do you need the loan?'

'To expand. I want to buy better fireworks and do more ambitious displays. I have dreams about the shows I can put on, but I can't afford to make them come true. And with two thousand pounds I can buy a computer that will work the whole thing.'

Jane made a note of the name on the book: Wakeham's Wonderful Fireworks. 'How long have you been in business, Mr Wakeham?'

'Six months.'

'Then you don't have any audited accounts?'

He pulled a face. 'I show you the glory of the heavens and you ask for accounts.'

'Every decision I make has to be justified to head office, and I can't represent the glory of the heavens in my report.'

'Head office! Report!' he echoed scathingly. 'Look at that rain of pink and blue pouring down from the sky. Shall I tell you the wonder of fireworks? You have to look up to see them. Most people never raise their eyes from the earth in their lives. The world, to them, is black and white, until I show them colours so vivid that they can't be ignored. Oh, all right, if you want figures, here are some figures.'

With an almost comical change of mood he set some typed sheets before her. To Jane's surprise the figures were efficiently set out and seemed thorough, with everything precisely costed. It was unfortunate that they only went back six months, but they suggested another side to Gil Wakeham apart from the madman.

'Tell me something about your background, Mr Wakeham. What jobs have you done in the past?'

She had the impression that the question had disconcerted him. He shrugged and looked uneasy.

'What do my past jobs matter? It's my talent for the present job that will decide how well I'll use your loan.'

'A loan that you still have very little chance of obtaining, let me remind you.'

'All right, I was born in London. I've done a bit of this and that. I've worked with figures. Those accounts are properly done.'

'Yes, they are. Is there anyone who could vouch for you, act as guarantor?'

He set his chin. 'No one that I'd care to ask. I want to do this independently.'

'You're making this very difficult for me, Mr Wakeham. I have to feed this data into a computer. The only thing a computer would do with what I've got so far is die laughing.'

'Computers don't laugh,' he said glumly. 'That's what's wrong with them. People laugh. And they sing and cry and gasp at my shows. And then they go away feeling happy. What would computers know about that?'

'That's all very fine, but I need something more solid than your airy-fairy imaginings.'

'Airy-fai—? May you be forgiven!'

'May *you* be forgiven for wasting my time,' she said with some asperity. 'This is a bank, not Santa's grotto.' Realising that she was allowing annoyance to ruffle her smooth surface, she took a deep breath and tried again. 'Do you have any collateral? What about your stock?'

'I've got about two hundred pounds' worth of fireworks at the moment, but since I'll be firing most of them tonight they're not much use as collateral. You might call them diminishing assets.'

'What about your caravan? Is it worth anything?'

'Tenpence. I bought it third-hand. It keeps breaking down and I have to repair it myself.'

Jane threw down her pen in despair. 'I find it hard to believe that you actually had the nerve to come here with these proposals.'

'There's my talent and hard work. Don't they count for anything?'

'Unfortunately they can't be represented on paper.'

'And if they can't be represented on paper they don't exist, do they? Miss Landers, I pity you.'

'Then you're impertinent as well as irresponsible.'

'I pity you because you can't lift your head from the figures.'

'It's one of the requirements of my job,' she said frostily.

'You're far too young and beautiful to be eaten alive by this place, with its functional desk, computer screen and plain walls.'

'They are *efficient*,' Jane said in her crispest voice.

'Efficient. God help you! Is that all there is in your life?'

She knew it was madness to let him tease her into an argument, but she couldn't help it. There was something volcanic about him, like a life force that drew her on in spite of herself. 'My life is none of your business, but I'll tell you this. It's built on strong values and stability, things you seem never to have heard of.'

'On the contrary, I've heard all too much about them, as though they were the only things that mattered. And what do they boil down to? The everlasting pursuit of money—'

'It was the pursuit of money, Mr Wakeham, that brought you in here.'

'*Touché*. But I only want money to turn it into something beautiful.'

'A firework display,' she said dismissively. 'Really!'

'An imaginative display can be a work of art.'

'You have the nerve to compare yourself to an artist—'

'I'm more of an artist than whoever made those *incredibly* tasteful prints on your wall. Did you know that they're chosen by head office for their restfulness? In other words, their blankness, their nullity. Art should jolt you out of yourself and make you cry out with wonder. It should make the sky light up, and in that sense, yes, I'm an artist.'

'Well,' Jane said in a voice intended to terminate the interview, 'I think that's all I—'

'I can make you see the universe the way you've never seen it before,' he went on as if she hadn't spoken. 'I can show you colours bursting from the heavens in showers of glittering rain. I'll bet there's no glitter in your life at all.'

'I'm an official of the bank,' Jane said flatly. 'My life isn't supposed to glitter.'

'But what about your heart?' he asked, giving her a sudden, piercing look.

'My heart does not belong in this discussion, any more than you belong in my office.'

'I wonder where your heart does belong?'

'That's enough. Will you please leave?'

'If I leave now I shall know I've failed.'

'You *have* failed. Kells Bank can't possibly give you a loan.'

'I'm not talking about a loan, I'm talking about *you*, a woman trapped in an underground cave. If I could bring you out of that cave I would show you wonders.'

She was about to rebuke him when something in his voice seemed to vibrate through her. She met his eyes. It was a mistake. Their look told her that he wasn't talking about fireworks any more.

'Wonders,' he repeated in a voice that had mysteriously softened. 'Magic. Do you know about magic?'

'I—no.'

'No. For you, there's only one life, the prosaic here and now. But what about the other world, where marvellous things happen? If you live without any contact with that world, you don't really live at all. And your upright gentleman friend, with his tie and his sense of responsibility, does he show you magic?'

'That's quite enough,' Jane said firmly. 'I'm sorry, Mr Wakeham. I just can't agree to this loan.'

'Don't decide now,' he said, apparently oblivious to her words. 'Come and see my work. I'm doing a display at the end of the county show tonight. See if the radiance and glory don't change your mind.'

'Nothing will change my mind,' she said with a touch of desperation. Was there any way of having the last word with this man?

'I'll see you tonight, then,' he said.

At the door of her office he shook her hand. Instantly she had a sensation as though a sparkle had communicated itself from him to her. She could feel it like an electric charge, shimmering through her until her whole body glowed. She almost snatched her hand away.

'Goodbye, Mr Wakeham,' she said firmly.

When he'd gone she took a deep breath. Her flesh was still tingling with memory. She looked around at her office, her place of triumph as she'd always thought of it. But now it seemed strangely drab. While he'd talked the walls had vanished, revealing beauty and vast horizons, but now the walls were there again, pressing in on her, like—she resisted the thought but it pushed through anyway—like a prison cell. Jane closed her eyes and gave herself a little shake to clear her head.

The door opened and Mrs Callam peered round it. 'I just had to come and say thank you,' she said. 'Of course I wouldn't disturb you while you were with that handsome young man.'

'I didn't think he was particularly handsome,' Jane said stiffly.

'Oh, but of course he was. Handsome and *so* charming, just the way a young man should be.' The old lady had gone pink and her eyes shone.

'Looks and charm are all very well,' Jane said, 'but surely what matters is a man's inner worth?'

Mrs Callam made a face. 'I've had two husbands, my dear, and you can take it from me that inner worth, while all very well in its way, is not the whole of life.'

'I don't think looks and charm are the whole of life either,' Jane said firmly. 'In fact, I don't think they matter at all.'

Mrs Callam regarded her with pity. 'I don't know what's come over young women today,' she said. 'No standards. No ideals. No sense of values.'

CHAPTER TWO

DINNER was perfectly organised and presented, as dinner with Kenneth always was. At seven o'clock precisely he'd collected her from her smart little flat, and driven her in his softly humming car to Wellhampton's most expensive restaurant. There the head waiter had greeted them as known and valuable customers, and Jane's favourite aperitif had been served instantly.

She was dressed with discreet elegance in a black silk cocktail dress, adorned by a single strand of flawless pearls. As she'd walked into the restaurant, heads had turned in admiration.

Here she was able to relax, secure in familiar surroundings and Kenneth's courteously expressed admiration. He was thirty, although he looked and sounded older. A heaviness, both of body and manner, had settled over him while he was still a young man. Unbidden, images of a lean, lanky frame began to flit through Jane's mind. Gil Wakeham was five years older than Kenneth, yet his mischievous charm made him seem—

Jane pulled herself together, wondering what had got into her. 'I always enjoy coming out with you, Kenneth,' she said firmly. 'I really do.'

'My dear,' he said with slight surprise. 'I'm delighted, but do you need to be so fierce about it?'

'Was I?'

'You said it as though making a policy statement.'

'I just think that perhaps I don't tell you often enough how much I appreciate you.'

He grinned. 'I'll remind you of that the next time I need a loan.'

'Don't let's talk about loans tonight,' she said edgily.

'It was only a joke. But I apologise. I was forgetting.'

'Forgetting what?'

'That you're not just a bank manager but also a beautiful woman.'

The words were fine, but strangely they hit a wrong note. Nothing about Kenneth was spontaneous, she realised, unless he was talking business. His gallant speeches sounded as though someone had pushed the correct button. She wondered why she'd never noticed it before.

'How are you doing with the preparations for your grandparents' golden wedding?' he asked.

'Pretty well. Mind you, the real work doesn't fall on me but on my brother James and his wife. They've got a house big enough to hold all the family, so they found themselves appointed hosts.'

'You're really going to have everyone there?'

Jane nodded. 'Absolutely everyone, including my uncle Brian who went to Australia years ago. The real problem is keeping it a secret. Sarah and Andrew think they've been invited for a small dinner, and they'll walk in and find nearly a hundred people there.'

'I can never get used to the way two such dignified people let their grandchildren call them by their first names.'

'Years ago they were Grandad Andrew and Grandma Sarah, to distinguish them from all the other grandparents in the family. As we grew older it just got shortened.' Jane gave a reminiscent chuckle. 'I'll never forget the day my brother Tony tried shortening Andrew to Andy. He soon got put in his place.'

'So I should hope. Your grandparents must be proud of their family. Five children, eighteen grandchildren, and not a bad apple among the lot.'

'What a funny way of putting it.'

'I only meant that the law of averages would indicate that one or two among so many should be less than satisfactory. Instead of which there isn't a single dud. Banking and law are the two professions that are the backbone of this country, and every one of you has gone into one or the other.'

'You're forgetting Tony, who had a go at acting.'

'Ah, but he came to his senses.'

'Yes, I suppose so. I've never felt he was really happy since he joined a bank.'

'Well, he hasn't climbed to your heights and I doubt he ever will, but he's solidly established, and a credit to the family.'

Kenneth took a sip of the excellent wine he'd ordered, and sat back to consider. 'Married for fifty years,' he mused. '*Happily* married. I'll never forget the first time you took me to dinner with them; your grandfather told a funny story about a rabbit, and your grandmother watched as though she was hanging onto every word.'

'I know,' Jane chuckled. 'You'd never guess that she'd heard that story a thousand times. He tells it whenever they have new guests, and Gran always laughs as though she's hearing it for the first time.'

'There you are. Wifely devotion. Mutual support, good times and bad. Security, dependability. The things that matter.'

Jane smiled. 'What about love? Doesn't that matter?'

'Of course. People ought to marry, so that they've got something to help them survive the rough places.'

'You make marriage sound like an assault course,' she complained.

'Life is a bit of an assault course,' Kenneth observed. 'Choosing your partner for the right qualities is vital. The important things are the ones that last.'

'Yes, but the things that don't last can be important too.'

'Such as?'

'Well—a burst of fireworks for instance. It's all over in seconds, but it could leave you with the memory of beauty.'

'Hmm! In my opinion beauty lies in great art, not cheap ephemeral displays. I don't underrate the importance of art to the soul. A great picture can inspire you for the workaday world—' he sipped his wine reflectively '—not to mention appreciating in value.'

'But looking at a picture is an ephemeral experience, isn't it? You can't stand there looking for ever.'

'No, but you could buy a print.'

'An incredibly tasteful print,' Jane couldn't resist saying.

He patted her hand. 'If you chose it, my dear, I know it would be incredibly tasteful.'

'That might be just what was wrong with it,' she murmured.

'Pardon?'

'Nothing,' she said hastily. To change the subject she asked him about business. Kenneth owned a prosperous building firm, specialising in conversions.

'Taking a stall at the county show was a good move,' he said as the main course arrived. 'Derek, who's running it, says there's been massive interest.'

'That's wonderful,' she said politely.

'I knew I was right to hold out for a good position. They tried to fob me off with a stall near the funfair, but I wasn't having any of it. In my opinion having a funfair at all was a great mistake.'

'People like to make a day out for the family.'

'But that's what it shouldn't be. A lot of deals get done at these shows. Money changes hands. Contracts are set up. What does a funfair have to do with it? And fireworks? I ask you!'

He continued in this vein throughout the meal. Jane listened to him with half an ear and made the appropriate responses. As they sipped their coffee Kenneth looked at his watch and took out his mobile phone. 'The show's nearly over. I'll just call Derek and ask him how things went today.'

'Why don't we go over there?' Jane said impulsively.

Kenneth beamed. 'That's very decent of you, my dear. I could have a useful chat with Derek, and we may want to discuss financing with you.'

It was dark as they went outside. A few minutes' drive brought them to the ground where the stalls and marquees were set up. As Kenneth headed for the car park Jane noticed a caravan under some trees. On the side, large letters proclaimed 'Wakeham's Wonderful Fireworks', but there was no sign of the owner.

They left the car and walked the short distance to the show. Everywhere there was a cheerful blaze of artificial light against the black velvet of the night. They soon reached Kenneth's stall. Derek was deep in conversation with a client, which ended, after a few minutes, with an arrangement to meet the following week to finalise matters.

'Jolly good,' Kenneth said when the customer had gone. 'I hope you've had plenty like that.'

'I haven't stopped since this morning,' Derek said. 'Those new brochures you ordered—'

The two men plunged into a discussion, occasionally turning to Jane for confirmation of some financial detail. She answered with half her mind. The other half had suddenly become unruly. It persisted in noting that the firework display was due to start in ten minutes.

A young couple approached the stand and began examining leaflets. Within minutes Derek had persuaded them that they needed an extension to their house. Jane listened to the familiar phrases: 'investment for the future'...'enhanced value'... This was the language she knew, with which she felt easy.

But tonight an unfamiliar restlessness possessed her, and she wanted to wander through the show, seeing new sights. She tried to attract Kenneth's attention, but he was doing business, and at last she drifted away.

'Ladies and gentlemen, the firework display is about to start in the field behind the funfair...' The voice came from the loudspeakers.

She had no intention of going to watch, but the crowd surged towards the field and she found herself carried along. She arrived just as the first rockets whooshed up into the sky, leaving trails of golden glitter. The crowd oohed and gazed upwards, entranced.

Jane could see Gil on a raised platform, setting off fireworks by throwing switches that sent electrical charges along cables. The lighting from below made him seem enormously tall, and threw shadows over his face. He grinned with pleasure at some spectacular effect, and in the dancing shadows he suddenly had the aspect of a wizard. Jane watched him, fascinated by his strangeness and the dazzling power that seemed to stream from him.

He could set fire to the sky. He was magic. And her life had been without magic until this moment.

He touched off three rockets that shot up, one after the other, until, at their peak, they exploded into showers of golden rain. The crowd gave a soft 'Ah' that rose to a cry of delight as each separate light exploded again, filling the sky with multicoloured gleams that poured down.

More rockets. Up and up, bursting out at last into flowers against the inky blackness. Unbelievable colours. Not just colours, but shades of light. Luminous. Beautiful.

There was artistry, but there was also wit. After a particularly noisy burst of fire one squib, coming after the others, made a frantic 'pop' that caused the crowd to laugh.

Jane looked around her. As Gil had said, people were standing looking up, their eyes glowing, their mouths smiling. Children's faces were full of wonder.

And then it was over. The last light went out in the sky, and a soft sigh seemed to break from the crowd. Reluctantly they lowered their gazes, back to the earth and their everyday problems which briefly they'd been able to forget. Most of them had a dazed look, as though they'd been permitted a glimpse of heaven, and seen it snatched away.

Gil jumped down from his platform, landing almost in front of her. He was smiling. 'You did come after all,' he said eagerly. 'I was sure you would.'

'Mr Wakeham, it's purely by chance that I—'

'But of course it is. Thank heaven for chance! What would life be without it?'

'I don't know,' she said, smiling back at him. 'Perhaps you've discovered the secret.'

A boy of about eighteen had appeared beside them. 'I'll clear up for you, Gil,' he said anxiously. 'Please let me.'

'All right, Tommy. You know where the bucket is. Do a good job.'

'And can I come and help you tomorrow?'

'No,' Gil said firmly. 'Go to the job centre tomorrow. Get a proper job.'

'But I want to do this,' Tommy protested, 'like you.'

'Hoppit!' Gil told him, never taking his eyes from Jane. Tommy pulled a face but went away without further argument.

In answer to Jane's enquiring look Gil said, 'Tommy's a local youngster who keeps trying to attach himself to me. I can't afford to hire him full time, but I let him do odd jobs. He's gone to search for unexploded fireworks. We make them safe in a bucket of water. Come on.' He took her hand and began to walk away, drawing her after him.

'Where are we going?'

'To get some tea. I'm parched.'

He stopped at a van where tea was being dispensed in plastic cups, and bought some for her and for himself. In her present mood it tasted better than the expensive wine she'd been drinking earlier in the evening, a lifetime ago.

A strange feeling, which at first she didn't recognise, pervaded her. It was as though a glowing delight had started in her heart and inched its way out to the extremities of her body. She was alive with it, tingling with it. It was like no other feeling she'd ever known, and at last she realised with a shock that it was pure, total happiness.

It came from being with him—this awesome creature who could create marvels. She remembered him as he'd looked on the high platform, a sorcerer brooding over his power, casting a spell over her, filling her with lightness.

Then she checked, wondering at herself. What had got into sane, sensible Jane Landers to make her indulge such a fantasy? He was just a man who'd performed a few clever tricks with gunpowder, and she was no child to be dazzled by them. But the feeling of happiness remained.

'Gil, there you are!' A plump, middle-aged man was making his way towards them.

Gil introduced them. The man was Councillor Morton, the organiser of the show. 'Wonderful performance,' he said. 'Your best ever. You must keep a vacancy for us next year.'

'If I'm still in business by then,' Gil said.

''Course you will be. They'll be flocking to book you. Here's your cheque, and if you'll just sign there...'

When he'd gone Gil caught Jane's suspicious eyes on him. 'I swear I didn't plan for you to overhear that,' he said, hand on heart.

'Hmm. I wouldn't put it past you. Don't tell me that remark about going out of business wasn't meant for me.'

'Well—maybe that one. But look.' He showed her the cheque, which was for two hundred and fifty pounds. 'Not bad, eh?'

'How much of that is profit, and how much will go on materials for the next performance?'

'Oh, stop being so practical,' he begged.

'Stop being practical! And he wants the bank to lend him money!' Jane observed to no one in particular.

'Now you've seen my work, what do you think?'

'I think it's wonderful. And you *are* an artist, but—'

He stopped her with a light touch on her mouth, which caused a faint, sweet tremor to go through her. 'Not now,' he said urgently. 'Say the "but" later. When was the last time you were at a funfair?'

'Oh—years ago.'

'Come on, then.'

Without giving her time to object he seized her hand and raced towards a ride labelled 'The Snake'. Next moment she was sitting with him in a narrow car and the attendant was fastening the metal bar across them.

'You're outrageous,' she laughed. 'I never do this sort of thing.'

'All the more reason to do it now.' He seized her hands. 'Forget being a bank manager for tonight. Just be a child and enjoy surprises the way children do.'

And suddenly it was obvious to Jane that this was the way life ought to be lived. She couldn't think how she'd wasted so much time not understanding such a vital truth. She squeezed his hands in return, and let out a little gasp as the car began to move.

The ride was circular, with two bumps followed by sharp dips. As they went into the first dip Jane clutched Gil's hands more tightly. Then she partly recovered her poise and seized the steel bar that protected them. She had to brace her feet to stop herself sliding about, and that too seemed amusing. She spent her life maintaining a dignified demeanour, and it was like taking a holiday to be undignified for once.

'Hold on, I'll steady you,' he said, and put his arm about her, his hand holding the bar next to hers. Thus encircled, she should have felt safe. But safe was the very last thing she felt. Power flowed from the magician, charging his body with an electricity that she could feel in her own. She was mad to be sitting here like this with him. A sensible woman would escape as soon as possible.

But she didn't seem to be a sensible woman any longer. The next moment a canvas hood rose from the inner side of the snake, swung overhead and down, enclosing them in darkness.

Fool! she thought. Now she was trapped with this madman, and since he evidently had no sense of shame he would probably take advantage of her helplessness to kiss her. But the moments stretched on and on with no advance on his part. She could feel his warm breath against her neck, but he didn't try to come any closer, and after a few moments the hood swung back. The car slowed and stopped.

'Come on,' he said. 'The fair closes in an hour and we have a lot to do.'

'But—'

'Hurry. Time's flying past. Can't you feel it?'

She gave up trying to protest and let him take her where he would. He bought them both lurid pink candy floss and they wandered through the funfair, munching it. They rode on the Ghost Train and clutched each other in mock terror, screaming and laughing. Then they had a duel to see who could toss the most rings over bottles, which Jane won triumphantly.

'You cheated,' Gil complained. 'That last ring didn't go all the way down, but the stall manager pretended it did because you flashed your beautiful eyes at him.'

'Jealous,' she mocked. 'Bad loser!'

'All right. Just tell me what you're going to do with a three-foot balloon shaped like a hammer.'

'This,' she declared, and bopped him on the head with it.

He grinned and took possession of her trophy, presenting it to a passing child. 'I feel safer now. Come on, let's have hot dogs.'

'My treat this time.'

'It'll have to be. All I have in the world is that cheque, which is useless unless you can cash it for me.'

'Not right this minute, no.'

'And you call yourself a bank manager! It would serve you right if I took my custom elsewhere.'

This struck her as terribly funny, and she laughed all the way to the stall. They had hot dogs washed down with cherryade, followed by chips and ice lollies.

'You're not dressed for a funfair,' he observed, looking at her elegant clothes.

'I didn't mean to come here. I dressed for dinner with Kenneth.'

'Who is where?'

'Oh—I lost him somewhere,' she said vaguely.

'Well done. Do you want to find him again?'

'Not tonight. I want to go on the big wheel.'

She began to move off but he grasped her arm. 'Hey, steady on. I'm not sure you ought to go on the big wheel dressed like that. You'll be cold.'

The cheerful craziness that had been bubbling up inside her for the last hour finally burst onto the surface. 'What is this? You're the man who believes in the pleasures of the unexpected, aren't you?'

'Yes, but—'

'Well, I came here with no idea at all of going on the big wheel, so it's clearly what I ought to do. It's your own philosophy.'

'A version of it—'

'I hate a man who doesn't practise what he preaches, and I'm going on the big wheel.'

'In that flimsy dress it just isn't common sense.'

Jane rounded on him, eyes flashing. 'I have practised common sense all my life,' she said, 'and tonight I'm having a rest from it. Understood?'

At once Gil clicked his heels and gave her a rigid salute. 'Yes, ma'am. Anything you say, ma'am.'

'Fool!'

She paid for two places and they took their seats side by side in the chair. As they swung up high over the fairground Jane began to understand Gil's doubts about her dress. They higher they rose, the colder she grew. Then they'd reached the top of the circle and were swinging down again. As they neared the ground Gil pulled off his jacket and wrapped it around her. The warmth was blissful.

'Thank you,' she said gratefully. 'You were right.'

He grinned wickedly. 'The wizard man is always right.'

Up, up, and up, till they were at the very top again. And there they stopped. And waited. And waited.

'What is it?' she asked with a touch of nervousness. 'Why aren't we going down?'

'They're probably letting someone else on down below. We'll move in a minute.'

But they didn't, and it began to occur to Jane that she disliked heights. Every movement made the chair rock wildly and she became horribly conscious of how little there was below.

'It's all right,' Gil said gently. 'Forget what's below. Think of what's above. Look up at the stars.'

Tentatively she did so, and felt his arm like steel beneath her neck. 'Sometimes I dream of sending my fireworks right up to the heavens,' he murmured. 'And I'll create a show like no one's ever seen, and the stars will be mad at me because I can play them at their own game.'

'If anyone can do it, you can,' she said with a sigh.

'I'll do it. I'll invent colours—pinks and blues, greens, gold and violet—all glowing and shimmering.'

'That'll make the stars really jealous,' she murmured. 'They've only got white.'

She felt his laughter as much as heard it. 'That's right. To challenge the heavens themselves. Just think of the glory of it!'

It was nonsense, but sitting here at the top of the wheel, with the earth far below them and only the singing air around them, she felt her fear evaporate and her spirit take wing. Gil's vision was so intense that it carried her up until she too could feel that to challenge the heavens would be a glorious thing.

She sensed his arm tighten about her. His hand was under her chin, turning her face gently to him. The touch of his lips was feather-light on hers, but it was enough to make the chair beneath her vanish. She was flying, floating in another world where the stars were a million colours, all exploding together. She watched, entranced, as they zipped and whirled around the sky, singing strange songs that took their music from her heart.

Somehow her head was on Gil's shoulder and she was yielding herself utterly to his kiss. She clung to him. Far away, in another life, she was trapped on a high wheel, and frightened. But in the warm, beautiful place to which he'd taken her there was no fear, only delight.

His lips were firm, teasing and caressing hers, enticing but not demanding. This was Gil as she'd first seen him, not only a wayward spirit but also a rock of kindness. She relaxed, knowing that he could keep her safe.

But even at that moment she sensed something else in his kiss—a powerful, dangerous masculinity that thrilled her. Gil was more than a light-hearted drifter. He was a man with a fierce possessive instinct. He was reining it back now, to reassure her, but she could still sense it there, promising, enticing, warning her not to dismiss him lightly.

He tightened his embrace. Jane gasped at the sensation of his mouth moving urgently over hers, speaking more eloquently than his words had ever done. Gil had talked of wonders, and she'd thought he meant only fireworks, but there was wonder to be found here in his arms. It dazzled her and opened up new vistas, beckoning her on...

The sounds of laughter and applause broke into her dream. Startled, she looked up and realised that they'd reached the ground and a smiling crowd was regarding them.

'How did we get down here?' she asked, dazed.

'The wheel started to move while we were otherwise occupied,' he said with a smile.

She tried to read his face, to see in it whether she'd imagined the explosion of light between them. Had he been as caught up in passion as herself, or had he merely tried to distract her from her fear? His smile was almost impenetrable, but she thought she sensed a new tension behind it, as though he too had been shaken.

He handed her out. Her legs were trembling, although whether it was because of her nervousness or the effect of Gil's kiss she didn't want to ask. It shocked her to have to acknowledge that she'd been so lost in him that she hadn't noticed what was happening to her, and suddenly she had a sense of danger.

'Thank you for your jacket,' she said, returning it to him.

'Give it to me later—' he began to say.

'No, really—I must be going now. I didn't mean to stay so late. Goodbye.'

'Wait, Jane—please.'

'I must go, I really must,' she said hurriedly.

She turned and fled. She was too honest not to face the fact that she was running away, fleeing the unknown, the magic, escaping back to her safe, ordered life.

She found Kenneth's stall but it was empty. Evidently he'd tired of waiting for her and gone home. Jane could hardly blame him. She went to find a taxi. All around her the show was beginning to close, and the lights were going out.

CHAPTER THREE

JANE awoke to the gloomy thought that she'd made a fool of herself. A total and utter fool. There was no excuse. She, who prided herself on her level-headedness, had succumbed to the threadbare tinsel of a clever showman.

She groaned as she remembered how easily she'd fallen into his arms on the big wheel. To her dismay the thought made the kiss live again: the firmness of his lips against hers, the sense of fierce, masculine purpose, so at odds with the casual persona he presented to the world. For a shattering moment she'd belonged to him as totally as a young girl experiencing her first kiss, and in the chill light of dawn the memory shamed her. He was everything she distrusted and disapproved of. Yet his embrace had blotted out the world as no other man's embrace had ever done for her.

Now she could see his strategy clearly. This morning he would march into the bank to cash his cheque, confident that he'd charmed her enough to wheedle a loan out of her. And she'd almost fallen for it.

She had a virtuous breakfast of black coffee and grapefruit, the very thing to wipe out the memory of candy floss and cherryade. Then she called Kenneth and apologised for her defection of the night before. 'I bumped into a man who wanted a loan,' she said. 'I'm sorry for not coming back to you. I hope you weren't too worried.'

'I must admit it was a bit awkward,' he admitted. 'We're packed with orders, and I'm going to need to expand. It would have been handy to have an answer about the finance straight away.'

'Your credit is good. There should be no problem.'

'If I could just run through it—'

'It's better if we talk when I'm at work,' she said, feeling that she couldn't endure listening to him now. 'My secretary will call you and make an appointment.'

As she drove to work she made stern resolutions. This must go no further. She would instruct her staff that when Gil came to the bank they were not to involve her. As soon as she reached work she summoned Harry to her office.

'I want you to take particular note of this,' she told him in her crispest voice. 'If a Mr Gilbert Wakeham presents a cheque drawn on the local council, please make sure that—' She stopped and drew a sudden breath. Luminous colours were chasing themselves across her consciousness. Up in the black sky the stars laughed and danced with their rivals.

'Yes?' Harry asked, staring at her.

'Please make sure that—that you send for me.'

'Is it a large cheque?' he asked, making notes.

'Two hundred and fifty pounds.'

Harry frowned. 'For an amount like that you don't normally—'

'Please do as I ask, Harry,' Jane said crisply. 'And make quite sure that everyone understands.'

'Yes, Miss Landers.'

She tried to concentrate on some work. By lunchtime there was no sign of Gil. Jane cancelled plans to eat out and had a snack in her office. As the afternoon wore on he didn't appear, and at three-thirty the bank closed.

Jane worked mechanically for another hour before telling her secretary, 'I have to leave early today. Put the figures on my desk and I'll look at them tomorrow.'

She almost ran to her car, and in a few minutes was heading for the grounds where the county show had been held. She arrived to find the place looking desolate. The stalls had vanished, the marquees were in the process of coming down. The funfair was being packed onto trucks ready for the next venue. Jane swung the car round to the place where Gil's caravan had been parked.

It had gone.

She pulled up sharply and sat there, feeling as if she'd had a blow in the stomach. The wizard had vanished into thin air, and suddenly she felt something akin to panic at the thought that she might never see him again.

'Looking for Gil, love?'

Jane jumped and turned to see the elderly woman who'd run the tea van the night before.

'Yes, I— He did say where he was going but I forgot to note it down.' She sounded as awkward as a schoolgirl, she realised, and she had a horrid feeling that she was blushing.

'Hawley,' the old woman said, naming the next town. 'Some bloke's giving a big party for his daughter's birthday.'

'You don't happen to know where in Hawley?'

The woman frowned while Jane held her breath. 'Chadwick Street,' she said at last. 'Or was it Chadwick Road? Or maybe it was Chatterham Street. One of them, anyway.'

It was thirty miles to Hawley but it felt like three hundred. As Jane drove she lectured herself sternly. She ought to leave the matter here. If the wizard had really vanished, good riddance to him and his dangerous enchantment. She must stop the car and turn back now. She put her foot down on the accelerator.

She arrived just as the shops had closed, making it impossible to buy a map. A passer-by directed her to Chadwick Street, but there was no sign of Gil. Another passer-by, alarmed by her distracted look, gave her directions for Chatterham Street. She made her way to it, silently pleading with the powers of magic to favour her this time.

At last she found herself driving down a wide, tree-lined street, with luxurious houses set back from the pavement, protected by semicircular drives. She went slowly, looking from side to side. Even so, she nearly missed Gil's van, parked in one of the drives, and had to brake sharply and reverse.

The squeal of brakes caused his head to appear from the back, and the next moment she jumped from the car and ran towards him. She was full of irrational joy but the words that came out of her mouth were far from joyful.

'You are the most irresponsible, inconsiderate man I've ever met,' she flung at him. 'Do you know how much trouble I've had finding you? How *dare* you take off without a word to me?'

He blinked. 'Pardon?'

'Do you think business is conducted this way? How am I supposed to give a loan to a man who disappears without warning?'

'But you're not going to give me a loan,' he reminded her. 'You said so.'

Jane drew a deep breath. 'That is entirely beside the point.'

'It seems to me to be exactly the point,' he said in bewilderment.

'Don't split hairs,' she said crossly. 'If this is your idea of persuading me that you're a worthwhile risk—'

'I thought we'd given that up as a lost cause,' he said innocently.

Defeated in argument, she simply looked at him in annoyance, delight and overwhelming relief.

'Come in,' he said, retreating into the caravan.

Inside she found a snug living space, covered in boxes full of fireworks, cables, hooks, a screwdriver, all the tools of his trade. Even so, it was a lot tidier than she would have expected from Gil.

'Let me look at you.' He put his hands on her shoulders. 'Are you all right?'

'Of course I am. Why shouldn't I be?'

'The way you ran off last night worried me. I tried to follow you but I lost you in the crowd. Did you get home OK?'

After Kenneth's unconcern this was like balm to her heart. She tried not to be affected, but the kindly look was back in Gil's eyes and his warmth seemed to communicate itself through his hands on her shoulders, right through her body. He'd shaved today, but it didn't make him look any more respectable.

'Yes, thank you. I got a taxi without any trouble.'

'A taxi? You mean your boyfriend didn't drive you?'

'He'd given up waiting for me and gone.'

Gil opened his mouth as if to speak, changed his mind and shrugged. Like all his gestures it was eloquent, conveying clearly that if that was the kind of man whose company she chose there was no understanding her.

'I was concerned for you too,' she said. 'I knew you had no money except for that cheque and I thought you would come to the bank.'

'Oh, I found a few pennies down the back of the seat,' he said with a shrug. 'Enough to pay Tommy a little and fill up with petrol. I'll get a free meal from my employer tonight, and tomorrow I was going to come back and see you.'

So he hadn't simply driven off and abandoned her. Jane had to look away, lest her pleasure show in her eyes.

'You get the point I'm really making, I hope?' Gil continued. 'The idea is to impress you with my genius at making money stretch a long way. Now, how about a cup of tea before I have to start work?'

He set the kettle on the small hob, pulled down the table flap, and settled Jane on a sofa. The atmosphere was cosy and domestic, and a far cry from the shimmering enchantment of the night before. In contrast to her fears, he wasn't acting like a man who meant to trade on their passionate encounter on the big wheel. In fact he seemed to have forgotten the kiss altogether. For which, she told herself firmly, she was devoutly thankful.

He was about to pour the tea when there was a knock on the van, the rear door opened, and a man's head appeared.

'Glad to see you've arrived,' he boomed.

'Good evening, Mr Walters,' Gil said politely.

Dan Walters had a superficially genial manner but hard eyes, which he flickered over Jane.

'You didn't say anything about bringing an assistant,' he remarked suspiciously. 'We settled the fee. I don't pay extra for two.'

'I wouldn't dream of asking you to, Mr Walters,' Gil said with a hint of irony.

'As long as that's understood. I'll show you where to bring your things round the back.'

Jane was about to protest that she wasn't Gil's assistant, but Dan Walters had already turned away to call to his wife. 'Brenda, the firework man and his Girl Friday are here. Open the gate for them.'

'Girl Friday!' Jane exploded in a whisper. Gil was rocking with laughter. 'It's not funny,' she muttered.

'It is,' he protested, choking. 'It's no good telling him the truth now. Once he gets an idea in his head nothing will shift it.'

Jane soon discovered the truth of this. Walters returned and eyed her with disapproval. 'You're not very practically dressed, are you?'

'Mr Walters, I am not—'

'I made it clear to Gil that he'd have to do all the work. I've got no time to help. I didn't hire a dog to end up barking myself.'

'I know that but I am *not*—'

'I've got a son who's mad about engines. He's about your size. Bren, have you got a pair of Jerry's overalls handy? Chuck 'em out here.'

It was a few moments before Jane could recover her voice, and by that time Walters was thrusting the overalls at her. Luckily they'd just been laundered and she gave up further protest, merely casting Gil a sulphurous glance that dared him to comment. But he too was beyond speech.

She changed in the van and followed Gil round the back to the large garden. From a storage place beneath the van he'd pulled some long metal pipes and he was busy fixing them together into a pyramid with rungs. He handed Jane a screwdriver and nodded briefly to her, telling her to get to work. Within a few minutes she'd discovered another aspect of Gil Wakeham. She'd met the charmer, the madman and the romantic. Now she met the slave driver.

Once he was absorbed in his work, nothing mattered but getting the result he wanted. He made her hold the pyramid together while he tightened nuts and bolts, and when she dropped something he said crisply, 'Come on, we haven't got all night.'

'Oi!' she said indignantly.

He gave her his delightful grin. 'Sorry. Forgot.' The next moment he was giving her orders again.

When the pyramid was built he attached to it a length of electric cable, interspersed with fireworks at three-foot intervals. But this time when Jane tried to help he discouraged her with a shake of his head. 'Don't fool with it,' he said. 'These things aren't toys.'

Well, at least, she reflected, now she could acquit him of trying to overwhelm her with charm.

In the house the party began. Outside dusk was falling. Gil produced a large torch and handed it to her to hold for him. 'Please,' he remembered to say after a moment. Jane regarded his bent head, his face frowning in concentration, oblivious of her, and it came to her with a start that she was enjoying herself.

As the light faded further the party spilled out onto the lawn. The young people appeared to be in their late teens or early twenties, and they had an aggressive self-confidence. One of them called to Jane, 'Hey you, boy.'

She stared at him.

'Hey, *you*.'

'Don't distract him,' Gil yelled. 'He's a stupid lad. I won't use him again.'

'You won't get the chance,' Jane muttered. 'How dare you?'

'You can always walk out in high dudgeon,' he suggested wickedly.

'Not for the world.'

'All right. We're ready now,' Dan Walters bawled.

The last time Jane had seen Gil's show she'd been enchanted. This time it was a different experience, one of darting here and there, having instructions barked at her. Gil wasn't intentionally impolite. It was simply that, as he'd said, he was an artist. Michelangelo too, Jane reckoned, had probably been a bit brusque while painting the Sistine Chapel.

'Hold this,' Gill yelled. 'Now back off and flick that switch when I tell you. Back further, *further*. Damn, I need more rockets. There's a box on the bed. Go on.'

'What?' she yelled, trying to make herself heard through the noise overhead.

'Hurry up and get it.'

'Yessir.' She ran to the van, found the right box and dashed back as if her life depended on it. For the briefest flash of an instant she wondered what on earth she was doing. The only thing she knew for sure was that she was having the time of her life.

The finale was a cacophony of rockets. The din was so awesome that Jane put her hands over her ears. In the flickering light Gil grinned at her while his hands moved fast, touching off switches here and there, making the heavens a blaze of light and noise.

Suddenly, there was silence. The last rocket fizzled out. The spectators rubbed their eyes. There was applause and murmurs of approval, but Jane sensed less of the wonder that had greeted the performance last night. These people were too superficial for wonder. She heard

Dan Walters say, 'I told him I wanted the best, and I got it. Always insist on value for money.'

It was praise of a sort, but Jane knew a spurt of anger that Gil's talent should be wasted on such a vulgarian. Didn't these people realise—?

'Hey, come on,' Gil urged her. 'It's time to pack up.'

She helped him dismantle the equipment and carry it to the van. While he went hunting for unexploded fireworks Jane packed boxes away. At last he returned, and as they were locking the storage space a large woman in an overall appeared. 'I was told to bring you this,' she said, holding up a paper bag.

Investigation showed the bag to contain sausage rolls, sandwiches and various fancy cakes, evidently party leftovers. To these the woman added a small bottle of mineral water.

'It looks a bit skimpy for two of you,' the woman observed. 'But *he* said he was only expecting one.'

'And Mr Walters is a man who doesn't give a penny more than he agreed,' Gil said gravely.

'That's it, dear. If I was you I'd eat up before he asks for it back.' She departed, radiating gloom.

'Well, you heard her,' Gil said. 'Let's get eating.'

In the caravan they set the rolls on the table. 'So much for the free meal from your employer,' Jane observed. 'I can't take any of this from you. There's barely enough for one.'

'Nonsense. I always share with the hired help.'

A demon seized her. In an excruciating accent she demanded, 'Well, ain't yer gonna pay me, guv?'

'Pay you?' he demanded. 'What impertinence! I let you sleep under the van and eat the scraps the dogs leave, don't I?'

They laughed together. 'Let me make the tea,' she said.

'Sit down, woman. I'm particular about how my tea is made. Start dividing the goodies, but remember, the lemon tarts are mine. You can have the ham sandwiches.'

As they had supper Jane said, 'Isn't he supposed to pay you?'

Gil grinned. 'I made sure of getting paid in cash before we started. Walters may not be a fool about money, but neither am I. I've met his sort before.'

'You mean they get out of paying you?'

'If they can.' Gil's reflective grin held a world of meaning as he added, 'Not any more.'

There was a thump on the van door, and Dan Walters' head appeared. 'There you are!' he said triumphantly, pointing at Jane. 'Come on. Get 'em off!'

'I beg your pardon?'

'Jerry's overalls. Give 'em back. Thought I wouldn't notice, didn't you?'

'Mr Walters,' Jane said primly, 'I assure you I'd completely forgotten I was still wearing your son's overalls—'

''Course you had. And that noise is a convoy of pigs flying past my head. They're new, them overalls. Cost a pretty penny too. I know your kind. Fly-by-night. Live in a van. Here today, gone tomorrow.'

Gil buried his head in his hands.

'If you will kindly leave, both of you,' Jane said in an arctic voice, 'I'll change my clothes.'

Gil pulled himself together, stepped outside the van and closed the door, but not before Jane heard him say, 'We'll wait here together, and seal off her exit in case she tries to make a run for it in Jerry's overalls.'

Jane's lips twitched.

When she was changed she felt more like her normal self. She returned the overalls to Walters, who remarked, 'Best be off now. You're blocking my driveway.' He departed without another word.

Gil got back into the van and surveyed her. 'You look like a bank manager again.'

'Yes, I'm afraid I do.'

'I suppose this is where we say goodbye.'

'But aren't you coming to the bank tomorrow?' she asked in dismay.

'There's really no point. I can cash the cheque anywhere, and I'm sure you don't want me bothering you any more.'

'But what will you do?'

'I've got work lined up all summer. I didn't mean to suggest I was starving. I only needed money to create a better performance.'

'With a computer.'

'And loudspeakers so that I can accompany every show with the right music. Think what an effect it would make!'

Jane had one of those blinding moments that come to people who know they're at a crossroads. She could let the wizard go driving off into the night in one direction while she took another, knowing she might never see him again. Or...

She snatched at her bag, rummaged in it and sat down at the table.

'What are you doing?' Gil asked.

'Giving you a loan,' she said breathlessly. 'It's what you wanted, isn't it?'

'Yes, but—' He stared at the piece of paper she'd thrust into his hand. 'Jane, this is one of your own cheques. You can't—'

'Yes, I can. Gil, I can't possibly give you a Kells loan. But I can lend you the money myself.'

'But I can't let you do this. It's too risky.'

'According to you yesterday it's as safe as houses.'

'Yesterday I was talking to a bank manager. Now I—'

'Yes?' She was suddenly full of breathless hope.

'Now—you're a friend. I can't take money from a friend.'

She had a mad inspiration. Diving into her bag once more, she took out the 'formidable' spectacles and perched them on her nose.

'Is that better?' she demanded.

He gave a shaky laugh. She had the feeling that she'd totally disconcerted him.

'Bless you for your faith in me,' he said. 'I can't tell you what it means to have a real chance of my dream—'

'No sentiment,' she commanded him sternly, from behind the glasses. 'I'll charge you the full banking rate of interest.'

'Certainly, Miss Landers.'

'You'll receive paperwork tomorrow. Where will you be?'

'I have to call on my suppliers in the morning, but I'll be back in Wellhampton in the afternoon. Same place as before.' He looked at her. 'Jane—that is, Miss Landers—would you please take those glasses off? There are some things I just can't do while you're a bank manager.'

'What?' she asked, removing them.

'This,' he said, taking her in his arms.

She'd expected it, hoped for it, but still she was taken totally by surprise. It wasn't like last night when he'd been inhibited by their situation. Nothing inhibited him now. This was an earthbound kiss, telling of his desire, the hot, hungry need of a man for a woman. This was the Gil who was used to giving orders, silently commanding her to respond to him. Jane yielded in helpless delight.

She knew that she'd never before understood passion. She hadn't then discovered this fierce, driving longing for a man whose whole person enchanted and mesmerised her. She'd thought of herself as calm and patient, a woman whose mind ruled her heart. But her senses acknowledged no rule. They roared out of control with every touch of his lips and hands, demanding more, demanding everything.

How could she be patient when her flesh was clamouring for him? It was almost scary, like finding that an unknown woman shared her body, a woman who recognised none of the insipid certainties that ruled Jane Landers' life.

She saw his face hovering above hers, and knew that his passion had risen as swiftly as her own. 'Gil...' she whispered.

Her voice seemed to recall him to the real world. Gradually his arms slackened. She found she could breathe again. 'I think...' he said unsteadily. 'I think—'

'What?' she murmured, through a haze.

'I think you'd better put your glasses back on again. We'll both be safer that way.'

Reluctantly she drew back, accepting his good sense even while her heart protested against it. She didn't want to be sensible. She wanted to fly up and touch the stars. At the same time she knew she wasn't ready for that next step. And Gil, the madman, had been prudent for her.

'Oh, dear,' she sighed.

'I know, darling,' he said gently. A glint of his usual humour illuminated his tense features. 'But there are some things we can't do in Dan Walters' driveway.'

That thought brought her down to earth. 'No,' she said with a shaky laugh.

'When we have the world to ourselves, in some lonely spot by a stream—'

'Don't,' she begged. 'It sounds too beautiful.'

He saw her to her car. She'd managed to recover some of her poise, and before she got in she said, 'Gil, promise me something.'

'Anything.'

'Open an account at some other bank. Don't bring that cheque into Kells. I could never look my staff in the eye again.'

He laughed and kissed her lightly. 'Promise,' he said.

As she drove home Jane found herself thinking of her grandmother, the matriarch who, with her husband, had been the core of the family for decades. What would that staunch lady say if she knew that her favourite grandchild was throwing her cap over the windmill?

In her mind Jane tried to talk to her. I know it's not the way I was brought up. He's not the kind of man you taught me to admire, but—it's the way his eyes laugh.

She gave up. Sarah, with her stern standards of responsibility, would never understand.

At last Jane reached her apartment block and took the lift up to the third floor. As soon as she stepped out onto the landing she knew something was wrong. There was a bar of light under her front door, and she was sure she hadn't left any lights on. She turned her key cautiously.

'There you are at last,' said a familiar voice.

'Sarah!'

Her grandmother's dumpy figure rose from the sofa and came to welcome her, arms outstretched. 'Sorry about coming into your flat when you weren't here, darling, but I didn't know how long you'd be. Your neighbour had a spare key, and he let me in.'

'That's fine. You know you're always welcome, but I wish I'd known. I could have got ready for you.'

'No need to fuss about me,' her grandmother assured her. 'A roof, a bed and a crust is all I ask.'

Jane suppressed a smile at this theatrical way of putting it. She hoped Sarah hadn't found out about the golden wedding party. It would be a shame to spoil the surprise.

Then she noticed several suitcases, and knew a small buzz of alarm. 'Sarah, what is it? What's happened?'

The little woman drew herself up to her full height and set her chin pugnaciously.

'I've left your grandfather.'

CHAPTER FOUR

FOR a moment Jane just didn't take it in. 'You've what?' she echoed, in a daze.

'I've left him. I've been saying for years that I would, and now I have.'

'But—you can't *leave* him.'

'Why not?'

'Well—for one thing, you're over seventy. And for another you've been married to him for nearly fifty years.'

'You don't have to tell me. Fifty years listening to that silly man make the same jokes day in, day out. I don't know how I've stood it.'

'But what happened to make you suddenly decide?'

'We had people to dinner last night, and he told the story about the rabbit, and I suddenly knew that if I had to listen to it again I'd start climbing the walls. So today I packed my bags and left, which is what I should have done years ago. It's not too late to live my own life.'

Jane relaxed slightly. At least there didn't seem to have been a major quarrel, just a case of the fifty-year itch. 'Let's have some supper,' she said. 'While it's cooking I'll make the spare room up for you, and we'll have a good talk.'

'You don't mind my dumping myself on you, do you, dear?' Sarah asked.

'Darling, you can stay for ever. It's just that this has knocked me all of a heap. Does Andrew know where you are?'

'It's none of his business where I am,' her grandmother declared rebelliously. 'And don't you go telephoning him. I've escaped and I don't want anyone spoiling it.'

'Escaped?' Jane was startled. 'You don't mean that.'

'Don't *you* start telling me what I mean. I've had enough of him doing it. I said escaped and I meant escaped. You try living with the same man for fifty years, and see if it doesn't feel like a gaol sentence.'

'But you love Andrew. Don't you?'

'I didn't say I didn't love him,' Sarah explained patiently. 'It's just that right now I can't stand the sight of him.'

Jane opened her mouth and closed it again. This was too much for her to take in. She felt as if the stable, ordered world she'd always known had been turned upside down.

While they had a light meal she tried to find out more. 'What did Andrew say when you left?'

'Nothing. He wasn't there. I left him a note.'

'Didn't you say where you were going?'

'No. And you're not to call him.'

'But Sarah—'

'Let him stew.' The light of battle was in her grandmother's eyes.

'You don't sound a bit like yourself,' Jane said, feeling thoroughly unsettled.

'You mean I don't sound like you've always thought of me,' Sarah said at once. 'A very different thing.'

'Yes, I suppose it is,' Jane said, much struck by this revelation.

To her relief Sarah went to bed soon after that, declaring that she'd had a tiring day—'but a very enjoyable one, my dear'.

'Enjoyable?' Jane echoed, aghast. 'Frightening the life out of poor Andrew?'

'Poor Andrew, nothing! Do the old fool good to have a surprise.'

When Sarah was asleep the first phone call came. It was Jane's elder brother George. 'Sarah's gone missing,' he said worriedly.

'It's all right. She's with me.' Jane briefly recited the evening's events.

'And you haven't called Andrew?' George echoed, aghast.

'She told me not to.'

'But surely you realise that Sarah isn't exactly herself?'

Jane had been thinking the same thing, but hearing it said out loud annoyed her. 'George, if you're suggesting that Sarah's mind is wandering merely because she's fed up with the story about the rabbit, then it's you that's taken leave of your senses.'

Loftily he ignored this. 'I shall certainly call him.'

'Do. But tell him not to come rushing over here. Sarah needs time.' She hung up, wondering why she'd never realised how pompous George was before.

It seemed that rushing over there was the last thing on Andrew's mind. He called ten minutes later, to ask, 'Is she all right?'

'She's perfectly all right—'

'Good.' He put down the phone.

Jane waited. After a precisely calculated minute, the phone rang again. 'I'm not talking to her,' he declared without preamble.

'That's fine, because she's not talking to you,' Jane said, exasperated.

'Well, I'm not talking to her. You can tell her that.'

'I can't tell her anything. She's fast asleep.'

'Asleep! How can she sleep when our marriage is in tatters? I always said that woman had no heart.'

'When she wakes up, do you want me to give her a message?'

'Yes. Tell her I'm not talking to her.'

The line went dead.

Torn between a desire to laugh and an equal desire to bang her head against the wall, Jane stared indignantly at the phone. The moment she replaced it, it rang again. It was her sister Kate.

'George tells me...' she began at once.

After that it never stopped. The news that Sarah was staying with Jane raced around the family, and every one of them called her to express their shock and offer advice. Their words varied, but in the end they were all saying the same thing. The fixed point in their ordered world had shifted, leaving them stunned and bewildered.

It was nearly two in the morning when Jane finally took the phone off the hook and went to bed. Although tired, she lay awake for a long time, wishing she could talk to Gil. She was sure his free spirit would give him a different outlook on the situation.

She overslept and woke to find Sarah, fully dressed, setting a cup of tea by her bed. From the kitchen came the delicious smells of breakfast. 'Andrew called last night,' she said.

'I'm not talking to him,' Sarah said at once.

'Don't worry, he's not talking to you,' Jane said, wondering if she'd woken up in a kindergarten.

Over breakfast Sarah said, 'I'm going to London today. I need some new clothes.'

'London's a very tiring place,' Jane objected. 'Hadn't you better—?'

'No, I hadn't better,' Sarah said firmly. 'I'm seventy, not a hundred and seventy.'

'But there are some lovely shops in Wellhampton.'

'Jane, dear, I've endured fifty years with one stick-in-the-mud. Don't tell me I've escaped merely to find another.'

'Stick-in-the-mud?' Jane echoed, outraged. 'Me?'

'If you're not careful. You became serious much too young.'

This was so close to what Gil had said to her at their first meeting that Jane knew a twinge of dismay. 'Seriousness is the family trait,' she reminded Sarah defensively. 'And who's responsible for that?'

'Your grandfather. Don't try putting the blame on me.'

Jane was left speechless.

She drove her to the railway station. 'I'll be home in time to cook you a good solid supper,' Sarah promised, and vanished before Jane had time to explain that she never ate heavy meals.

She broke her busy morning schedule to call Andrew at the comfortable riverside bungalow where he and Sarah had lived for the last ten years. His voice was boisterously cheerful. 'I've bought a boat,' he announced. 'A nice little launch. I've always wanted one.'

'I didn't know that.'

'There's lots of things I've always wanted, and now that I'm free I'm going to have them.'

'Won't a boat be a bit strenuous for you?'

Andrew chuckled. 'I'm not going to sail it. I'm going to entertain young women on it.'

Jane drew a slow breath. This was worse than she'd thought. 'Sarah may have something to say about that,' she said, trying to make a joke of it.

'She's got nothing to say. She ended our marriage, not me. Best thing she ever did. Now I'm going to start enjoying myself. Wine, women and song, and no one saying, "Don't do that, it's bad for you!" Tell her I'll manage very well without her. Is she all right?'

'She's fine. She's planning to enjoy herself too.'

'I'm not interested. Don't say that woman's name to me.'

'All right, I won't.'

'She'll come running back. I'll bet she's sitting by the phone waiting for me to call right now.'

'No, she's gone to London to buy new clothes.'

'I told you, I'm not interested. If this is all you have to say I'm going to hang up. I've got a lady friend to entertain.'

Jane muttered, 'Heaven give me patience!' and set down the receiver.

She was half afraid that Gil wouldn't be there when she drove out to find him that evening. But to her relief she saw his caravan standing under the trees.

As soon as she knocked on the door his hand came out to seize her and draw her in. The next moment she was in his arms. 'I was afraid you wouldn't come,' he murmured against her mouth.

'I was afraid you wouldn't be here.'

Breathlessly he released her. 'Look,' he said, indicating the table. 'I spent the afternoon getting it ready.'

She gasped at the sight of the table elegantly laid for two. He'd clearly taken a lot of trouble. 'Oh, Gil, I can't.'

'Of course you can.'

'No, really—my grandmother is waiting for me at home, cooking supper. She turned up last night. She's left my grandfather and the whole family's in turmoil because we were planning their golden wedding party. She's buying new clothes and he's buying a boat to entertain young women—'

'Whoa, there! Calm down. You're not making sense.'

'None of it makes sense,' she said crossly. 'They're like a couple of children. He says he won't talk to her, and she says she won't talk to him. They're both in their seventies and they're practically saying, "Yah! Sucks! Boo!" to each other.'

Gil grinned. 'If they've lived together all these years they must be just about ready to say, "Yah! Sucks! Boo!"' he observed. 'They've probably said everything else a dozen times over.'

'Not a dozen. A thousand. Sarah says if she hears his favourite story again she'll start climbing walls.'

'I like the sound of her.'

'She's a darling. I have to put her first just now.'

'Does that mean I can't see you?' he asked, dismayed.

Jane was about to say that Gil was just the sort of man to give Sarah a fit when an idea came to her. If Sarah met Gil she would certainly disapprove of him, and begin to sound like herself again.

'No,' she said slowly. 'I think you should come home to dinner with me. Sarah always cooks enough for ten.'

'This is very sudden.' Gil gave her an impish grin that made her heart somersault. 'I'm not being set up for something, am I?' he asked.

'Of course not. It's just that—' She hesitated, unsure how to put it delicately.

'It's just that the sight of me will rouse her to a frenzy of horror and warn her of the slippery path she's treading,' Gil supplied.

'It's not exactly—like that,' Jane hedged.

'Darling, I could have a wonderful time watching you tie yourself in knots trying to explain—exactly—what it *is* like,' he said with a chuckle. 'But why bother? I don't mind being used as an awful warning. Will I be awful enough as I am?'

'Well, it's a pity you've shaved,' Jane said, examining him critically.

'I did it for your sake,' he complained. 'There's no pleasing some women. How do you want me to be? Drunk and disorderly?'

'Certainly not. Just be your normal self.'

'Will my normal self give her enough of a fright? Yes, of course it will. I perfectly understand.'

'I give up,' Jane said.

'In that case, shall we go?'

He picked up the wine bottle from the table and followed her out of the van. Jane used her carphone to tell Sarah they were on their way.

'How did she sound?' Gil asked when she'd hung up.

'Suspiciously cheerful. I can't wait to get home and discover what new pit she's opened at my feet.'

'Don't sound so disapproving,' Gil told her. 'She's old enough to do what she wants.'

'That's what she says,' Jane mused.

'The point is, she shouldn't need to say it.'

Halfway home he stopped off to buy a bunch of flowers. 'For my hostess,' he explained to Jane.

'Crawler,' she accused him amiably.

'Of course. It's the first rule in the Gil Wakeham school of survival. When faced with overwhelming forces, grovel. Besides, giving flowers to the hostess is the proper thing to do.'

'I know. But if you do the proper thing it ruins the view of you that I'm trying to present.'

'Not at all. I'm a ne'er-do-well who pinched them from someone's garden.'

'Can't you ever be serious?' she asked, exasperated.

'Whatever for?'

'I don't know. I used to know a thousand reasons for being serious, but suddenly I can't remember them.'

'Splendid. You're making progress.'

As they went up in the lift she checked his appearance. He was dressed as he had been the first day, in black leather trousers and a black sleeveless T-shirt that clung to his body, revealing its taut contours.

'Will I do?' he asked, reading her gaze perfectly.

Tremors of pleasure went through her at the hint of the devil in his eyes. 'Your hair's too tidy,' she said in a voice that shook slightly.

Immediately he ran a hand through his hair, untidying it. Unfortunately the tousled look made him even more wickedly attractive, but Sarah wouldn't appreciate that, Jane reflected with relief. With an effort she pulled herself together and opened her front door.

A delicious smell was wafting from the kitchen. They both sniffed appreciatively. 'Bangers and mash!' Gil said. 'Wonderful!'

'It'll be nothing of the kind. Sarah's a cordon bleu cook. Bangers and mash is beneath her.'

'Shame.'

'We're here,' Jane called.

A strange woman emerged from the kitchen. Jane was about to ask who she was and what she was doing here, when she gulped and realised this was her grandmother.

Gone was Sarah's grey hair. In its place was a subtle shade of honey, beautifully cut and shaped. Instead of her usual functional, unimaginative clothes Sarah was wearing an elegant navy blue and white dress, set off by discreet silver earrings.

'Sarah?' Jane gasped. 'I thought you were a stranger.'

'Oh, darling, what a lovely thing to say. Do you really like it?'

She turned, showing the dress from all angles. Somehow Sarah had managed to lose a lot of weight in one day. Her face, too, had been made up by an expert. She had a new elegance, which suited her, but she didn't look at all like Jane's grandmother. While Jane was wondering what to say, Gil solved the problem with one long, fervent wolf-whistle.

Sarah turned to him, beaming. 'You must be Gil. I'm so glad Jane brought you home to meet me.'

'So am I,' Gil said, his eyes on her. 'So am I.'

Under Jane's amazed eyes he gave Sarah an old-fashioned bow, and handed her the flowers. 'These are for you.'

'Oh, how lovely. It's so long since a man bought me flowers.'

She bustled away to put them in water, and Jane muttered at Gil, 'What do you think you're doing? That's not the way to scandalise her.'

'I thought my appearance alone was supposed to do it.'

'I don't think she's even noticed your appearance.'

'Come and sit at the table,' Sarah called. 'I'm famished, and I'm sure you are.'

'I've been telling Gil all about your cordon bleu cookery,' Jane said.

'I'm afraid I haven't had time for all that today,' Sarah said. 'You'll have to settle for bangers and mash. It's always been my favourite, but your grandfather didn't like it, so of course we never had it.'

'I love it,' Gil offered.

'Good, because there's plenty.' Sarah bustled into the kitchen.

'I wish you'd stay in the part,' Jane grumbled.

'Sorry, darling, but not even for you am I going to pretend not to like bangers and mash,' Gil said firmly.

Jane hurried into the kitchen to help with the serving. 'Gran,' she whispered, 'how did you lose all that weight so quickly?' Suspicion darkened her voice. 'You're not doing aerobics, are you?'

'Oh, stop sounding like an old woman,' Sarah chided her. 'I've got a really good foundation garment.'

'You never bothered before—for Andrew.'

'Andrew didn't like me to look pretty. As long as clothes are tidy and functional he thinks they're all right. He'd have a fit if he could see this.' She raised the hem of her dress to reveal a black, lacy petticoat.

'Wow!' said Gil from the doorway. 'Some chick!'

That should do it, Jane thought. It was a safe bet that no one had ever called Sarah a chick before. But instead of being horrified Sarah merely blushed prettily. 'Will you take these in, Gil, dear?' she asked, indicating the plates.

When Gil had gone Jane made a desperate attempt to retrieve the situation. 'I apologise for the way Gil's dressed,' she said. 'He didn't know he was coming here.'

'What's wrong with the way he's dressed?' Sarah asked.

'Well, it's a little unconventional for you.'

'My dear, when a young man is as delightful as that, he can wear whatever he likes. Now bring that bread-basket and let's make a start.'

A health-conscious dietician would probably have tut-tutted at the meal Sarah laid before them: thick fried sausages, frothy potatoes mashed with cream and topped off with butter. But it was delicious, and Gil's wine made it perfect.

'How did you two meet?' Sarah asked as he filled her glass.

'I came into the bank, asking for a loan,' Gil said. 'Of course Jane turned me down.'

'Why?'

'Why?' Jane echoed. 'Look at him.'

'I'm afraid I don't have time for all that boring stuff about the proper clothes,' Gil said, making a valiant effort to get back into character. 'Life's too short.'

'Yes,' Sarah said with a sigh. 'It certainly is.'

'But sometimes the proper clothes are important,' Jane urged.

'Not nearly as often as you'd think,' Sarah said. 'But of course living in a bank breeds the conventional viewpoint.'

'I don't actually live in the bank,' Jane pointed out.

Sarah gave her a disconcerting gaze. 'Don't you, dear?' Having reduced Jane to silence, Sarah smiled at Gil. 'I hope you're going to tell me all about yourself. What do you do for a living? I can tell it's nothing boring.'

'Fireworks,' he said. 'I go around the country giving displays.'

'How thrilling!'

'Of course, it's a bit of a risky life,' Gil said, aware of Jane's frosty eye on him. 'No proper home, just a caravan.'

'You live in a caravan?' Sarah asked, wide-eyed. 'That's wonderful! A different place every day, the horizon always changing, new people.'

'Right,' Gil agreed. 'I can't bear sticking around the same place too long.'

Once Sarah would have shaken her head at this, and words like 'immature' and 'volatile' would have hovered on the tip of her tongue. But she seemed entranced by Gil.

'It can't be much of a life, though,' Jane said, trying to get the conversation back on track. 'No roots, no family ties.'

'That's the best way to live,' Gil said cheerfully. 'Ties only tie you down. Give me freedom. Give me the open road.'

'Give me no sense of responsibility,' Jane said.

'Jane, dear, that wasn't very kind,' Sarah reproved her. 'I'm sure Gil does have a sense of responsibility.'

'No, I haven't,' he said at once. 'Life should be fun, that's what I say.'

'So do I,' Sarah said.

Disconcerted, Gil hesitated, but then returned to the fray. 'Families are all very well, but they tend to hold you back, always trying to tell you what to do for your own good, or what not to do. Who needs it?'

'No one,' Sarah said fervently. 'Take it from me, no one. You're not married, then, I gather?'

Gil winked. 'I run too fast.'

'I'm sure there are plenty of young women in pursuit,' Sarah said.

'Too many to count,' Gil assured her. 'I like it that way. Keeps them on their toes.'

Sarah leaned towards him conspiratorially. 'But Jane's the front runner?'

Gil considered. 'At the moment. But, as I always say, who knows what tomorrow may bring?'

'It'll bring you a kick on the shins in a minute,' Jane said indignantly.

Sarah and Gil looked at each other and began to laugh.

'I'm sorry, darling,' Sarah said, patting Jane's hand. 'But you didn't really think I'd be fooled, did you?'

'She did. I didn't,' Gil said, with the air of a schoolboy dodging blame.

'Jane's a dear,' Sarah confided, 'but just a little bit gullible.'

'When you've both finished,' Jane protested.

'I'm afraid I didn't carry it off very well,' Gil admitted.

'Too overdone,' Sarah said. 'It's obvious that you're not used to acting a part.'

'But I really do live in a caravan and give firework displays,' he said.

'Well, why shouldn't you?'

'No assets. No security. Only debts. Ask Jane.'

Sarah regarded her granddaughter fondly. 'I wouldn't ask my darling Jane anything. She knows all about figures and nothing about people.'

'Is that so?' Jane demanded.

'Yes, dear. Instead of trying to use Gil to alarm me, you should have told me how good-looking and charming he is.'

Gil sighed. 'At last, a woman who appreciates me,' he said soulfully, with a mischievous glance at Jane.

Jane fought to keep a straight face but couldn't manage it, and the three of them burst out laughing together. 'The two of you are impossible,' she said, defeated.

'All the most attractive men are impossible,' Sarah said. 'If I'd met Gil forty years ago I'd have left your grandad for him like a shot.'

'And I'd have made sure you did,' he said gallantly. He refilled the glasses and they all toasted each other.

'Now the next course,' Sarah said. 'Trifle and cream.'

'Mum would never let me have trifle when I was a child,' Jane mused. 'She said it would rot my teeth.'

'Then you must have a double helping now,' Sarah said.

As they ate she made them tell her the story of their first evening at the funfair, listening with her eyes aglow, like an eager child. She was even more delighted by the tale of the next day, when Jane had assisted Gil in his display, and loaned him money.

'I really am a con man,' he insisted, in a belated attempt to win Sarah's bad opinion. 'I parted Jane from her savings in double-quick time.'

'No security,' Jane agreed. 'It was the silliest thing I've ever done. Aren't you ashamed of me, Gran?'

'On the contrary, dear. It's a relief to know you can act recklessly, like other young women.' She smiled at Gil. 'Just fancy not knowing what tomorrow will bring.'

'Well, actually, I cheated a bit there,' Gil confessed. 'I've got a string of engagements fixed up over the next few weeks. I've got them written down somewhere.' He began to search in his pocket.

'When you've bought the computer, you must let me log them on for you, properly,' Jane insisted.

'What for? The back of an envelope does the job OK. Here we are.' He produced a scrap of paper and read from it. 'One wedding, one child's birthday, one display from a boat out at sea, one jar of pickles— No, that's another list. Well, there are a few more somewhere.'

Jane studied the list. There were dates but no place names. 'Do you remember where any of these places are?' she asked.

He shrugged. 'I expect I'll remember when the time comes.'

Jane gave up. For the rest of the meal she sat and enjoyed the sight of Gil and Sarah flirting outrageously. They drank coffee, and when they wanted some more Gil insisted on making it. While he was in the kitchen Sarah drained her wineglass and murmured, 'A real man of mystery.'

'Mystery?'

'This is a first-rate vintage. He may look like a rebel, but he has sophisticated tastes. I wonder where he acquired them?'

Gil returned before Jane could answer, and proceeded to serve them coffee as neatly as a waiter.

'It's time I was going,' he said at last. 'Mrs Landers—'

'Sarah.'

'Sarah, I haven't enjoyed an evening so much for years.'

'Come back any time,' Sarah said, and Jane could tell that she meant it.

'I'm just going to drive Gil back to the caravan,' Jane said. 'I won't be long.'

On the journey Gil couldn't stop talking about Sarah. 'What a doll! What a fabulous woman to have for a grandmother!'

'She liked you too,' Jane said with a chuckle.

'Sorry I couldn't stay in the part, but I wasn't very convincing, was I?'

'Never mind. It was a wonderful evening.'

At last she drew up next to the caravan. Gil looked at her, his eyes gleaming.

'Time to say goodnight.'

'Yes,' she sighed.

'And I'm off first thing in the morning.'

'Oh, no!'

'I'll be back as soon as I can, but it'll probably be a week.'

'Or perhaps the open road will beckon and you won't return at all,' she said, trying to sound casual. There was a sudden fear in her heart at the thought that he might really vanish into thin air.

Gil gently placed the tips of his fingers under her chin and lifted her face to his. 'I'll come back,' he said softly. 'You've got under my skin, and I can't forget you.' He lowered his lips to hers. 'However far I go, I'll come back to you—always.'

She couldn't speak, but her answer was in the eager response of her lips. She was falling in love with Gil. It wasn't wise. In fact, by all the standards of her life, it was madness. But she couldn't help herself. His kisses made her heart sing. The feel of his strong body pressed close to hers made her long to know him intimately, and the thought of being apart from him was unbearable. When he deepened the kiss she clung to him, trying to imprint the memory of it so deeply that it would last her while he was away.

At last he tore himself free. 'You'd better go home quickly,' he said. 'This is dangerous.'

'I love danger,' she said recklessly.

'I know, my darling,' he said, stroking her face. 'But you're not used to it yet. Now I'm going to get out of this car while I'm still strong enough to leave you. But I'll be back soon.'

She watched him walk away from her until he reached the caravan and waved. She waved back and drove away slowly, her heart already aching with their separation.

She let herself into the flat quietly, so as not to wake Sarah if she was asleep. But her grandmother was sitting up in bed, her eyes shining. 'What a wonderful young man,' she said as soon as Jane went in. 'So full of life!'

'He's very good entertainment,' Jane conceded cautiously.

'Oh, don't be so stuffy! And don't pretend you're not half in love with him, because you couldn't keep your eyes off him.'

'I was merely concerned in case you found his company too much. He's not the kind of man you're used to meeting.'

'No, worse luck!' Sarah said regretfully. 'I never get the chance to meet anyone like that. There's something positively Regency about him.'

'Regency?'

'Yes, flamboyant and blazing with life. Just think how he'd look in those buckskins they used to wear!'

'Buckskins?' Jane echoed, fighting to keep up.

'*Skin-tight* buckskins,' Sarah said ecstatically. 'Surely you've noticed what an attractive shape he has?'

'I think you must have had too much wine,' Jane said severely. 'You'll feel better in the morning.'

'Stop sounding like Andrew. In fact you're worse than Andrew. You sound like my parents. They'd have thrown your Gil out of the house.'

'He isn't my Gil, and *you* should have thrown him out of the house,' Jane said, feeling increasingly unsettled.

'Not for the world,' Sarah vowed. 'There are too few men like him.'

'You talk like Mrs Callam. She's had two husbands. The first, from all I've heard, was a pillar of the community. The second was a ne'er-do-well who spent most of her money. But he's the one whose picture she carries around with her.'

'Which proves my point.'

'What point? I've lost the thread.'

'Yes, Gil has that effect, doesn't he?'

'I'm going to bed,' Jane said firmly.

CHAPTER FIVE

THE week of Gil's absence seemed interminable to Jane. The colours of the world, so brilliant before, had faded into shades of grey.

Sarah settled in to enjoy herself. She went to beauty classes and bought new clothes with cheerful abandon. Jane could see now that her grandmother was still an attractive woman, and began to understand the impulse that had caused her to make a dash for freedom before it was too late.

Andrew telephoned every second day to enquire after his wife. 'She's doing fine,' Jane would tell him. 'Wouldn't you like to speak to her?'

'What for? I know what she's doing—spending money like water. I've just got my credit card statement. Just who is Madame Elaine?'

'Andrew says, who's Madame Elaine?' Jane relayed.

'She did this lovely job on my hair,' Sarah informed her.

'She's a hairdresser,' Jane told Andrew.

'A hundred and fifty pounds for a hairset?' Andrew yelped.

'It's rather more than just a set,' Jane said.

'For that much, I should think it's a whole new head.'

'That's what it looks like,' Jane agreed.

'And what did Beauty of Bond Street do for her?'

'Gave her a whole new face.'

'Do you realise that your grandmother is spending money like there's no tomorrow? Clothes, shoes—she's taken me right up to my credit limit.'

'Then she won't be able to spend any more,' Jane pointed out.

'Nonsense! I've never kept her short of money. She may be ungrateful and unreasonable, but I hope I know my duty to my wife, even if she doesn't know hers to me. You can tell her that I've paid off a thousand pounds, which I've no doubt she'll waste on another spending spree.'

'Why don't you tell her yourself?'

'I don't want to talk to her,' he snapped, and hung up.

'You're in the black again,' Jane told Sarah. 'Andrew's paid in a thousand pounds.'

'Oh, good! I can afford that new coat.'

Sarah had telephoned all her friends and soon garnered a mass of invitations. Jane's post was less interesting.

'What is it, dear?' Sarah asked one morning over breakfast. She'd seen Jane making a face at a letter.

'Just something from head office about my holiday entitlement,' Jane said. 'I've got two weeks left over from last year, and if I don't take them by the end of June I'll lose them.'

'Take them,' Sarah said at once.

'What time have I got? I've already pencilled in two weeks for this year, but I was thinking of letting them go as well.'

'Don't start doing without holidays,' Sarah warned. 'I've seen too much of what that leads to. Take the whole four weeks together and have fun.'

'I'm too new in the job to be taking four weeks at once.'

'Oh, how often have I heard that refrain?' Sarah exclaimed. 'I can't take time off for this reason or that reason. Over-zealousness has been the curse of our family. Don't let me see you fall victim too.'

A short time ago Jane's jaw would have dropped at this outrageous pronouncement. But by now she was getting used to Sarah's new self, and she merely put the letter away without comment.

It was a bad day at the bank. Jane surveyed the rising pile of work and wondered how she could even contemplate two weeks off, never mind four. It was eight in the evening when she returned home, and the flat was suspiciously quiet. She discovered why when she found a note from Sarah on the kitchen table.

'If your grandfather rings, tell him I've gone out on the town with my toy boy.'

Jane wasted no time wondering about the identity of the 'toy boy'. Gil must have returned. Her heart leapt, then fell again. He might have returned but he wasn't here, where he should be. He was out having fun with Sarah.

Slightly disgruntled, and trying not to admit it to herself, Jane settled to whatever pleasures could be found in a solitary omelette, washed down with mineral water. After that she spent the evening writing a report for head office. It was virtuous but definitely unrewarding. Her mind persisted in going 'on the town' with the two reprobates.

It was past midnight before they returned.

'Still up, dear?' Sarah enquired. 'You should be getting your beauty sleep.'

'So should you,' Jane replied indignantly. 'What time do you call this?'

'I call it twelve-thirty,' Gil said immediately. 'What time do you call it, Sal?'

'I call it twelve thirty-one, but we'll agree to differ.'

Laughing, they shook hands. Jane regarded them in despair. It was plainly useless trying to get through to a pair so enchanted with each other.

'I've had a wonderful time,' Sarah announced. 'Gil's shown me his delightful home—'

'And Sal cooked me the best meal I've ever had,' Gil supplied.

'Who, may I ask, is Sal?' Jane enquired, regarding him coolly.

'Why, me, dear,' Sarah said. 'We decided it suited my new persona.'

'Sal the Gal,' Gil said, his arm around Sarah's shoulders. 'The liveliest gal in town.'

'You ought to be ashamed, both of you,' Jane said, trying to sound severe.

'We are. We're very ashamed,' Gil said instantly. 'Aren't we, Sal?'

'You speak for yourself,' Sarah said robustly. 'I'm not ashamed. I've had the time of my life.'

Sarah was looking happier than Jane had ever seen her before. Her eyes were glowing, and she clutched a large bunch of red roses. 'Look what Gil bought me,' she said. 'I'll go and find some water for them.'

She hastened away, leaving Gil and Jane regarding each other. She tried to look stern, but the glint of wicked humour in Gil's eye was too much for her. Her lips began to twitch, and at last she gave in and laughed aloud.

'Did you miss me?' he asked.

'No, not at all.'

'That's a pity. I missed you all the time. Night and day. Especially at night.' He gave a heavy sigh. 'Still, if it's not mutual—'

'Gil, this isn't fair.'

'What's fairness got to do with it?'

'I refuse to answer that question. It's designed to trap me.'

He said nothing, only smiled at her, while her heart leapt and bounded and refused to be still.

Sarah returned with the roses in a vase. When she'd set it down she gave an exaggerated yawn. 'My, I'm tired. I think I'll go straight to bed. Goodnight.'

They bid her goodnight without taking their eyes from each other, and the moment she'd gone they were in each other's arms. All the ache of missing him was in Jane's kiss, and the pressure of his lips on hers told her that he felt the same. The magic was there again, making the room vanish, revealing the dark skies against which lights glittered and glowed. Catherine wheels spun madly, tossing off lights in ever increasing circles, rockets zoomed hither and thither. The heavens were full of light and joy. Her magician had returned and there was magic in the world again.

Yet mysteriously, while the enchantment shimmered, the sense of his powerful arms holding her tight gave her a feeling of total safety that she couldn't understand. It was like coming to the place where you knew you belonged, and recognising it as home, although it looked like nothing you'd ever imagined.

Reluctantly she freed her lips. 'All right,' she said unsteadily. 'I admit I've missed you these last few days.'

'Badly?'

'Yes, badly.'

'Me too. And it's going to get worse because I'm going to be away for several weeks. I told you I had a string of engagements, and since then I've added some more. I've got to go north and I won't have time to get back here between shows.' He tightened his arms and said eagerly, 'Jane, come with me.'

'But how can I?'

'You've got several weeks due off work. Sarah told me. We could spend those weeks together, just the two of us, driving around, giving shows.'

'Don't,' she begged. 'It sounds wonderful, but I can't possibly leave Sarah here alone.'

'It was Sarah's idea.'

'What? It's true she's been urging me to take time off, but I don't know that she meant me to become a gypsy for a month. Are you sure you didn't misunderstand her?'

'It's not me who's misunderstood her. It's her family, all these years. And she may not just be thinking of you. She might want some time herc alone so that she can enjoy herself in her own way, without you waiting up for her like a wrathful parent.'

'But what's she going to get up to while I'm gone?'

'Jane, my darling, that's simply none of your business. She may be seventy but she's in good health. Stop being the family representative and let her have fun.'

'I just feel that I ought to be urging her back to Andrew, where she belongs.'

'That's her decision,' Gil said firmly. 'Maybe she'll never go back to him. Have you thought of that?'

'Oh, no, it's impossible. Underneath everything she loves Andrew.'

'Does she? What about the other fellow?'

'What other fellow?' Jane stared. 'You're not suggesting that Sarah was ever unfaithful?'

'I don't know. It may have happened before she was married. But I'm sure there was someone.'

'Gil, what has Sarah told you?'

'Not much, directly. She spoke of her marriage very correctly, but I sensed a subtext. She never actually said she'd loved another man, but I'll swear there was someone who had her heart the way Andrew never did. Perhaps I'm wrong. I'm probably letting my imagination run away with me.'

But Jane was no longer as sure of that as she would once have been. She was realising that she'd never really known anything about Sarah. Maybe Gil, seeing her with eyes untroubled by family tradition, had seen her most clearly.

'I'd better be going now,' he said. 'I leave next week. Try to come with me.'

'It would be wonderful,' she mused. 'If only...'

He kissed her lightly, and was gone.

Jane looked in on her grandmother, and found her awake. 'I'm too excited to go to sleep,' she said. 'I've had such a time. You're so lucky! He's a delightful man. He treated me as gallantly as if I'd been a young girl. How many men would be so attentive to an old woman and never look bored?'

'Yes, he's a very nice person,' Jane agreed.

'Of course, it wasn't all for my sake. I'm a realist. It was you he wanted to talk about. But he was kind and generous to me, all the same. And so *thrilling*!' She saw Jane's raised eyebrows and added primly, 'There are some things that even an old woman like me is still aware of.'

'Really? Tell me,' Jane urged impishly.

'You know what I'm talking about. If a man has it, it's always there. Even if you're only discussing the price of fish, it's *there*. Of course,' she added wryly, 'some men never have it. Unfortunately, those are the ones a woman is usually condemned to live with. But—' she seized Jane's hand '—if you find it—oh, my dear, don't dismiss it as not worth having.'

Jane's hand closed over Sarah's. 'I just don't know,' she said slowly. 'I've been so confused ever since I met him.' She met Sarah's eyes. 'Gil said there was a man you loved once...' she ventured tentatively.

'Yes, of course he saw that. I should think he sees most things.'

'Then he was right?'

'Oh, yes.' A wistful note came into Sarah's voice. 'There was someone before I married Andrew. He was a fireworks man. Not literally, like your Gil, but in himself. He was an actor. At one time I wanted to be an actress.'

'I never knew that,' Jane said. But even as she spoke she was remembering Sarah's tendency to dramatise, her occasional theatrical comment. And Tony, her own brother who'd shocked the family by trying to become an actor—he was Sarah's grandson.

'It was in the forties,' Sarah said, 'when acting was still frowned on for a respectable young woman. My parents let me join an amateur company to get it out of my system. And I met him.' Sarah's eyes were suddenly alight with glorious memory. 'We were going to run away together and turn professional. For a time it actually seemed possible. But then—' She sighed as if returning to earth. 'My parents forced me to break it off. Parents could do that in those days. They said he was "unsuitable". He went away and I never heard of him again.

At last I married Andrew. He was in banking, and very suitable.'

'Oh, Sarah, did you love this other man very much?'

'Very, very much,' Sarah said softly. 'To me he was rockets, and golden rain, and coloured lights in the sky.' She gave a wry smile. 'But I had to give him up and marry a squib.'

'It's not very kind to call poor Andrew a squib.'

'A *damp* squib,' Sarah said firmly. 'He's been a good husband, according to his lights. He's worked hard, he's faithful, and in his way he's kind. But I've never forgotten my fireworks man. He used to shower me with red roses.'

'Like Gil?' Jane said.

'That's right. He understands. Every woman should have red roses when she's young.' Sarah patted Jane's hand. 'Go away with Gil.'

'If only I could,' she said wistfully.

'You can. You need only believe that you can. Go into work tomorrow and tell them you want four weeks off. Spend them with Gil.' A sudden earnest note infused her voice. 'Do it while there's time. Seize the chance. Don't spend your life wondering what might have happened—as I did.'

As soon as she got into work next day Jane called head office to put in for her holiday. She found herself talking to the secretary of Henry Morgan, an aloof, critical man, who had opposed her appointment to this job. The chance of his agreeing to four consecutive weeks was remote, and the secretary seemed to think so too, for her voice was frosty as she said she would call back.

After an hour the call still hadn't come, and she decided this was an ominous sign. The phone rang.

'Yes?' she said tensely.

'Mr Grant is here,' said her secretary. 'Can he see you?'

'Yes, send him in.'

Kenneth appeared, smiling. 'I don't have an appointment, but it won't take long,' he said. 'My mother wants you to come and spend your holiday with us.'

'That's very kind of her—'

'She knows how matters stand between us, and she's hoping everything will be finalised soon.'

'Hold on. You're running ahead of me,' Jane protested. 'Just how do matters stand between us, Kenneth?'

'I'm talking about our marriage.'

'Our *what*? It's news to me that we're going to be married.'

'But surely—I may not have actually gone down on one knee—'

'Or even mentioned it at all,' she pointed out.

'I thought we had an understanding. We're so right for each other—'

'Kenneth, I can't marry you. I'm sorry if you thought it was all settled.'

His smile never wavered. 'I don't mean to rush you. Don't give me your answer now. Spend some time at my home and when you see how well you fit in—'

'I can't marry you just because I fit in with your home.'

'I've expressed myself badly—'

'It doesn't matter. I'm going away with a—a friend.'

Kenneth's lips pursed. 'From the constraint in your voice I deduce it's a male friend.'

'Yes. A male friend.' A sudden rush of spirit made Jane add, 'He drives round the country giving firework displays. I'm going with him for a month.'

He stared. 'Have you taken leave of your senses?'

'Yes. Yes, I have. That's exactly what I've done. I've taken leave of my senses, and I'm very pleased about it.'

'But—this is totally unlike you.'

Suddenly Jane understood how Sarah felt. To have people telling you what you were like only made you want to shout that you weren't like that at all. But before she could do so Kenneth went on, 'You can't possibly take a whole month off in one go. Think of the damage to your position. I do hope you won't put your request through to Mr Morgan. I know him. He won't just refuse, he'll put a black mark against you for a frivolous attitude.'

Jane felt suddenly deflated. 'It doesn't matter, Kenneth. I simply can't marry you.'

He regarded her with patronising kindness. 'Well, you're not jilting me for this gypsy, are you? I don't somehow see you travelling the roads. Look, I can't stay. I just dropped in to give you Mother's message. I'll tell her you've made other arrangements, but we can fix something later. Goodbye, my dear. Don't do anything foolish like asking head office for four weeks, will you? Believe me, your reputation would never recover.'

He departed before she could voice her indignation. Then annoyance faded to be replaced by resignation. Of course the whole idea was mad. When Gil was with her his way of looking at life seemed the only possible one, but when he was absent reality intruded. The trip had been an impossible dream, and for yielding to it she would have a black mark against her.

She pulled herself together and called her secretary on the intercom. 'I'd like some coffee, please,' she said.

'Straight away,' came the secretary's voice. 'Oh, and by the way, head office called and said four weeks was fine.'

A week later Jane was standing in her hallway, surrounded by bags, wondering at the speed of events. When Gil had learned that she was coming with him he'd seized her up ecstatically in his arms. Sarah too had been thrilled, and had promptly embarked on a shopping spree—'to equip you properly, darling'. She'd returned with several pairs of jeans and casual tops, a thick, hooded raincoat and a pair of wellington boots. After the initial surprise Jane had realised that all this was more suitable than her elegant wardrobe.

Now she was ready to embark on what felt like an adventure. It would be just a few weeks travelling around the countryside in a caravan, but it was actually the most momentous trip of her life.

Gil appeared and carried some of her bags downstairs. Jane looked anxiously around at the flat.

'You haven't forgotten anything,' Sarah said, reading her face correctly. 'Go, and have a lovely time.'

Jane put her arms around her grandmother, but their embrace was disturbed by a voice in the doorway. 'Ah, I got here in time.'

'Kenneth!' Jane exclaimed. 'What are you doing here?'

'I came as a friend,' he said gravely. 'I've been concerned about you. Good morning, Mrs Landers.'

'I'm delighted to see you again, Kenneth,' Sarah said politely, if untruthfully.

'Please allow me to express my sympathy at the recent unfortunate events in your life, and to hope that time will make all well again.'

'Unfortunate events! Whatever are you talking about?' Sarah asked. 'I'm having a wonderful time.'

Kenneth smiled in perfect understanding, and murmured, 'So courageous. It eases my mind to know that Jane has you to care for her. I'm a little surprised that you should have sanctioned this hare-brained scheme, but—'

'I didn't sanction it, I encouraged it,' Sarah said firmly. 'I like Gil very much.'

Kenneth was a bit taken aback. 'Well, of course, if you've met him and approve—'

'Totally,' Sarah said. 'He's an excellent young man.'

Gil chose this moment to appear in the doorway. He took in the little scene at a glance, and a gleam of wicked humour lit up his dark eyes. A change came over his lean body as he leaned it casually against the door.

''Ere, are you comin', or do I 'ave to wait all day?' he demanded belligerently.

Kenneth turned and regarded him with horror. Gil was at his most bohemian, dressed in tight jeans and open shirt, with a pendant around his neck. Jane fought to keep a straight face.

'Don't keep a bloke 'anging abaht,' he commanded her.

'Kenneth, this is Gil. Gil, this is Kenneth,' Jane gabbled.

Gil ostentatiously examined his hands and wiped them on his jeans before extending one to Kenneth, who took it reluctantly, for the briefest possible time.

'That your car downstairs?' Gil demanded. 'Blue one?'

'I drive a blue Mercedes,' Kenneth confirmed.

'Nice bit of goods. Not knocked orf, is it?'

'If you mean by that is it stolen, then no, it certainly is not.'

'Give yer a grand for it?'

Kenneth turned to Jane. 'I thought better of you, Jane,' he muttered. 'Good day to you.'

The front door closed behind him.

'Gil, dear, that was very naughty,' Sarah reproved him tenderly.

'I know. But irresistible. He so plainly expected the worst. And when you told him I was an admirable young man what else could I do—?'

'Leave this instant, the pair of you,' Sarah commanded.

'Jane, are you ready?'

'Yes,' she said. 'Just a few last-minute— Sarah, are you sure you're going to be all right?'

'Perfectly all right, dear. Now do hurry up and go.'

'I've showed you how to work the central heating—?'

'Three times.'

'And what to do about the cistern?'

'Four times. Now go.'

'And the newspapers are—'

'Go!'

'I'm going, I'm going.' This time Jane made it as far as the door where Gil stood patiently waiting. 'And don't forget to—'

'Gil, get her out of here,' Sarah commanded.

Grinning, Gil took hold of Jane. 'What's this?' he demanded, feeling a bulge in her pocket.

'My mobile phone.'

'Leave it behind.'

'But it'll be so useful—'

'Yes, and I know what for: keeping in touch with the bank. Leave it. You don't want to talk to anyone who wants to talk to you. Here, Sal, catch!'

To Jane's indignation Gil tossed her phone to Sarah, who caught it neatly. 'Take her away, Gil,' she said.

Gil blew her a kiss and retreated, closing Jane's front door firmly.

'You've got a nerve!' she seethed.

'Sure I have.'

'Gil, I just have to check—'

'Leave it,' he said. 'Whatever you've forgotten will just have to stay forgot.' He propelled her irresistibly towards the lift.

'Hey!' she protested.

'If I don't take drastic action you'll be there all night.'

As soon as the lift door closed behind them Gil took her into his arms. She embraced him eagerly, joyful in the reassurance of his passion, and that closeness of the heart that linked them even more deeply.

'We can't kiss properly here, but let's make the most of what we can do,' he murmured against her lips.

'Yes,' she said blissfully. 'Oh, yes...'

Lost in delight, they failed to hear the lift doors opening, or the shocked gasp of the person who stood there. But at last something in the thunderously disapproving silence got through to them.

'Hello, Kenneth,' Gil said amiably, drawing Jane out of the lift.

Kenneth grasped her arm. 'I came to reason with you—to tell you that it's not too late—'

'Oh, yes, it is,' she said. 'It's been too late for a long time. This is what I was trying to tell you the other day. Goodbye, Kenneth. Forget me, and find someone worthy of you.'

Still in a happy dream, she let Gil guide her to the car. Another moment and they were on their way.

'That was shocking,' she mused. 'I should be ashamed of myself. But I'm not. Oh, this is going to be wonderful.'

'Darling, there's something I have to confess to you,' Gil said sheepishly.

'What is it?'

'Look in the back.'

Jane turned round and found herself eyeball to eyeball with a basset-hound. 'His name's Perry,' Gil said.

'You never said anything about livestock.'

'I wasn't sure how you'd react. You're not allergic to dogs, are you?'

'Now he asks me! No, I'm not allergic to dogs. I actually like them. He just gave me a shock.' She considered Perry's thick, muscular frame and short legs. His face was mournful, as though the cares of the world rested on his shoulders.

'He has a nice nature,' Gil assured her.

Studying the smooth brown head close to her own, Jane saw that Perry's eyes were intelligent and gentle. When she reached out a tentative hand he promptly dropped his chin into it.

'I never even knew you had a dog,' she said. 'How come I've never seen him before?'

'Oh, well—I've only just got him,' Gil said vaguely. 'In fact, he isn't really mine—except that I guess now he is.'

'Can you explain that cryptic utterance?'

'Not really. Let's just say that he's mine.'

'How did he get his name?'

'It's short for Pericles.'

Jane gave a hoot of laughter. 'Pericles? You called a dog Pericles?'

'I managed to shorten it to Perry, but he won't stand for anything else.'

One of Jane's bags, which Gil had tossed onto the back seat, contained sandwiches for lunch, and Perry was soon taking a determined interest. She tried to solve the problem by pulling the bag forward onto her lap, but this merely made matters worse. At last she unwrapped the sandwiches and fed them to Perry, and after that there was peace.

CHAPTER SIX

THE weather was overcast when they started the journey, but as they left Wellhampton behind the sun came out, flooding the countryside with golden light. It was like a promise of joy to come, and Jane's heart was light.

'We have two hundred miles to do today,' Gil told her. 'There's a county show, running for three nights, and we have to perform last thing each night. Today we'll just reconnoitre the ground, and decide where everything's going to go. I'll show you the charts where I plan things.'

'On the computer, you mean? By the way, you haven't told me anything about that computer.'

Gil suddenly became awkward. 'Well—actually—'

'Actually what?'

'When I went to my suppliers they had a new consignment of fireworks in. The very latest. Wait until you see the size of these rockets, the colours—they're out of this world. I'll be one of the first to have them, and it'll put me ahead of the field.

'The computer would have made it easier for me to set the display off, but it wouldn't actually have improved what the crowd sees. With these new rockets I'll have a better show. There was really no choice.' He added quickly, 'I didn't deceive you. I really meant to get the computer, but by the time I'd finished buying every firework in sight there wasn't any money left.'

'Don't apologise,' she said, laughing. 'You wanted the money to improve the display. It's up to you how you do it. And, as you say, bigger and better fireworks are the logical way.'

'You're an angel for understanding. It's just that—'

'What?'

'The show's more extensive, and takes a lot of putting together. In fact, it's about twice as much work—for both of us. I'm really glad you're with me.'

She eyed him. 'I see. None of that romantic stuff about moonlight, and how lovely to be alone with you, darling?'

'Of course not,' he said, shocked. 'You're here to be useful, woman. Didn't I mention that?'

'No, you overlooked that bit.'

They laughed together. Jane fell silent and turned sideways to enjoy contemplating Gil. He was already brown from working outdoors, and the sun caught his hair, bringing out its blue-black colour. It outlined his profile too, emphasising the high forehead, straight nose and stubborn chin. But it was his mouth that attracted Jane's attention. Mobile, firm and beautifully shaped; a mouth made for kisses, she thought happily. It looked what it was—warm, skilful and loving, a mouth that teased and delighted her.

And kisses were no longer enough. She acknowledged frankly that she wanted to make love with Gil, and discover if the silent promises in his lips would be kept. And soon, she knew, it was bound to happen. This beautiful male animal was all hers. At least, he was hers for the immediate future, and Jane, whose career had been built around the precision of graphs and forecasts, was content to look no further than the next few weeks.

'We should be thinking about lunch soon,' he said.

'Any idea what we're going to do?'

'Nope.'

'Lovely.'

At last they pulled into the yard of a country pub. It was an oak-timbered building, with hanging baskets full of flowers. Perry clambered out and looked eagerly around him. Gil hastily fastened a lead onto him.

'This is my treat,' Jane said firmly.

'Fine. While you're getting the food I'll take Perry over there,' Gil said, pointing to some woods. 'I'll have whatever's on the menu, plus an orange juice. All right, Perry, I'm coming, I'm *coming*.'

Perry loped off with Gil in tow, his arm at full stretch and getting longer by the second, Jane noticed with a chuckle. He was a powerfully built dog, with short legs and ears so long that they constantly got under his huge paws. Evidently his frame was mostly muscle, for Gil was having trouble keeping up, and no success at all in holding Perry in check.

Jane went into the pub and collected shepherd's pie and orange juice for them both. By the time she carried them out the other two had reappeared, but this time Gil was in front, and Perry seemed to be intent on getting back to the woods. Occasionally Gil would stop and appear to remonstrate with his companion. Jane couldn't hear what was said, but she could sense the determination on both sides. Perry's nose was twitching, and it was clear he'd been hauled away from some delicious scent.

Gil saw her looking at them and stopped to make a helpless gesture. It was a mistake. Perry took advantage of the moment to dash back in the other direction, nearly hauling Gil's arm from its socket.

It was Jane who saved the situation. Suddenly inspired, she hurried towards them, holding out the shepherd's pie. The result was all she'd hoped. Perry applied his brakes sharply, turned and headed for her. Jane backed until she'd reached the car, at which point Perry caught up, demolished the food with one gulp, and had to be restrained from eating the cardboard plate as well.

'Whose food was that?' Gil asked, rubbing his shoulder.

'Mine,' she assured him. 'This one's yours—*Perry*! Well, it *was* yours. Wait here. I'll get some more.'

'*I'll* get some more,' Gil said firmly. 'You can stay here with the hound from hell.'

'You said he had a lovely nature.'

'He does have a lovely nature. He also has the strength of an ox, the self-will of a child and no sense of responsibility.' He handed her the lead. 'He's all yours. I'm going for shepherd's pie.'

'Better get three portions,' she suggested.

Gil eyed Perry askance. 'You're right.'

'Poor darling,' Jane said, when Gil had gone. 'Fancy calling you the hound from hell! You were just following your instincts, weren't you?'

Mournfully he agreed, laying his head in her lap, and looking up with eyes that said he placed his trust in her. She scratched his head until Gil returned with more food.

'Perry's probably thirsty,' Jane said. 'Where's his water bowl?'

'I don't have one,' Gil said.

'How can you not—?'

'I've only owned him a few hours, and in all the rush of getting ready—'

'All right, I'll see to it,' Jane said. She fondled Perry's huge ears. 'Poor old boy. This man doesn't know how to look after you properly.'

She departed, leaving Gil gaping with indignation. The landlord produced one of his own dog's bowls, which she filled with water. Perry slurped happily until it was empty. Then he consumed the food Gil had brought him, begged a titbit from each of them, and lay down, contented.

When they'd eaten Jane looked around their living quarters. She'd seen them before, but now she viewed her surroundings with the eyes of someone who had to fit into them. At its best the caravan had probably been top-of-the-range, but that had been some time ago. It was spotlessly clean, but everything had a worn look, and she discovered that some of the doors needed careful negotiation before they would close.

Gil had cleared some space for her, and she hadn't brought many clothes, but she could see they were going to be pretty cramped. The table was a flap that folded up against the wall when not in use. On either side of it were cushioned seats, long enough to stretch out on. The tiny gas stove had two burners. There was a minute bathroom with a shower, but no sign of anywhere to sleep.

'At night we fold the table flap against the wall,' Gil said, coming in behind her. 'Then the sofas become beds. There's not much room between them, but it's enough to get in and out. OK?'

'Fine,' she said, trying to sound enthusiastic. Somehow, two single beds wasn't what she'd been expecting.

'We should get going, I think,' Gil said.

As he locked the caravan Jane asked, 'Where's Perry?'

'I left him asleep by the car.'

'Well, he's gone now.'

A search revealed Perry in the pub's rear gardens, wolfing down ice cream that was being fed to him by a crowd of children. Nearby a middle-aged man and woman regarded the scene indulgently.

'Poor creature,' the woman said. 'Whoever owns him obviously doesn't feed him properly.'

'Obviously,' Gil agreed. 'Three helpings of shepherd's pie was plainly inadequate. Come on, you disgraceful hound.'

In a few minutes they were on the road again, Perry snoring loudly in the back. Their destination was Dellbrough, a midland town surrounded by farms. As they reached the ground where the county show was to be held they could see tents already standing, and trestle-tables being set up inside. A man guided them to an open space at the rear of the show, and showed them where they could park.

'I'm Jack Hastings,' he said when they'd got out of the car. 'The council sent me to show you around and make sure you had everything you need. Is this site right for you? We followed the instructions you sent.'

'Perfect,' Gil said, surveying it. 'Well clear of trees and buildings. Did you arrange for the scaffolding, as I asked?'

'There'll be some lads along with it tomorrow. Did you have an exact plan?'

Gil produced a paper, covered with lines and squiggles. 'It's like this...' he began.

Jane put Perry on a leash and they went exploring together. They found a small row of shops where she bought bowls for his food and water, cans of dog meat, biscuits, and a rubber ball. With the important matters seen to she was free to concentrate on food for herself and Gil. A quick glance had revealed that his larder was sparsely stocked, so she bought steaks, salad, wine, coffee, and milk, plus tea, bacon and eggs for the following morning.

It was half an hour before she returned, expecting to find Jack Hastings gone, but the two men were still deep in technical discussion. Jane watched, half listening, and fascinated by the change that had come over Gil. She knew he could act like a dictator during a performance, but this was something else. A natural authority seemed to have settled over him, and he gave his instructions quietly, but like a man who was used to being obeyed. It was a sharp contrast to the devil-may-care face he presented to the world, and to her. Once again she realised how much of him was a mystery.

When Jack Hastings had finally gone Jane said, 'Now for some supper.'

'Not just yet,' Gil said, squinting at his paper. 'There are things I want to show you.'

Jane and Perry exchanged glances and moved closer together. 'We're hungry,' she said firmly.

Gil sized up the opposition. 'In that case I give in. But there's hardly any food; I'll have to get some.'

'There's plenty of food. Where do you think I've been this last half-hour?'

He looked surprised. 'Did you go away?'

Jane ground her teeth. 'He didn't notice we'd gone,' she informed Perry. 'How do you like that?' Perry sighed mournfully. 'I agree,' she said with feeling.

'Sorry,' Gil said with a grin. He followed her into the caravan. 'What can I do to redeem myself?'

'Take these,' Jane said, unpacking the things she'd bought for Perry. 'You feed him. I'll feed us.'

While she was cooking he got out some papers, covered in signs and symbols, explaining that they were his blueprints for displays. When she told him his steak was ready he set the papers aside, but only by a little.

Things weren't going as they should be, Jane reflected ruefully. They ought to have clinked glasses and gazed into each other's eyes. It was true that Gil gave her his warm smile, and praised her cooking, but his conversation was about fireworks, and he kept having new ideas that had to be scribbled down before he forgot them.

Jane let herself be drawn in, genuinely fascinated. But there was a little twinge of disappointment in her heart that couldn't be suppressed. She hadn't come here for fireworks. She'd come for Gil. Yet he seemed strangely remote from her.

After supper he behaved beautifully, doing his share of the washing-up and putting everything away tidily. He showed her where the bedding was, and said with elaborate casualness, 'Perry and I will just go out for a little constitutional while you—er— Well, come on, boy.'

He clipped on the lead and the two of them vanished, leaving Jane indignant. Far from removing her garments one by one in a romantic seduction scene, he'd made sure of not being around until she was safely under the covers. She made up both beds with unnecessary force, working off her frustration by punching pillows.

When she'd finished she began to look around again. In one drawer she found a booklet about the caravan. It contained a detailed description of how to convert the two beds into one double bed. It was really quite easy, but Gil had hidden the booklet away in the back of a drawer. Seething, Jane shoved it back in and slammed the drawer shut. The knob fell off in her hand.

When Gil returned she was already in bed with her eyes closed. She would have opened them if he'd shown any interest in her, but he seemed preoccupied with settling Perry for the night. But the dog disliked the cramped conditions and kept trying to get outside. At last the two of them vanished, and after a few minutes Gil returned alone. He changed into his pyjamas behind a carefully drawn curtain, got into his bed, and turned out the light.

'What have you done with Perry?' Jane demanded after a moment.

'Laid a blanket under the caravan for him. He likes the open air.'

'Suppose he wanders off?'

'He can't. I've attached his lead to the caravan. Are you comfortable?'

'Perfectly, thank you.'

'The bed's not too short?'

'Not at all.' Just too lonely, she thought sadly.

'And you're warm enough?'

'I'm warm enough.'

'That's fine, then.'

'Yes, it is.'

'Goodnight.'

'Goodnight.'

Despite her indignation Jane was tired, and she soon began to doze off. Her mind was full of Gil—how it would feel to be taken into his arms, her body vibrating with passion.

With a shock she opened her eyes to realise that the vibration was real. The whole caravan was shaking rhythmically.

'What's happening?' she asked.

In the darkness she could hear Gil's rueful chuckle. 'I'm afraid it's Perry. There's not a lot of room under there, so we're going to know every time he makes a move.'

'But what's he doing?'

'I rather think he's scratching himself.'

Jane muttered a very rude word. So much for dreams of love.

'It's all right, he's stopped now,' Gil said. 'Goodnight.'

'Good*night*!'

Jane awoke to the sensation of a warm, heavy body pressed up against hers, through the blankets. Opening her eyes, she found herself gazing into another pair of eyes, full of soulful adoration.

'Hello,' she said, scratching her companion's enormous ears. 'I thought you were sleeping outside?' Perry sighed and snuggled closer. 'You're not going to make a habit of this,' she informed him. 'You're lovely, but you're not the one I want to cuddle. Off with you!'

She pulled a cotton dressing gown on over her night-dress and stepped outside. It was still early morning. The sun was just up, the dew was still on the ground, the air was cool and fresh. And there, wearing only his pyjama trousers and dancing barefoot in the damp grass, was her beloved. Jane watched fondly as he threw up his arms to the sky as if embracing the day, the whole world.

Perry bounded over, barking excitedly, and man and dog danced round each other, yodelling in unison. When he saw Jane, Gil raced back to the caravan. 'Look at it,' he told her eagerly, indicating the whole field. 'Isn't it wonderful?'

'It's only a field,' she said with a laugh.

'*Only a field?* Where's your vision? That's like saying an artist's canvas is only a bit of old material. *This* is my canvas. This is where I'll paint my pictures.' He grabbed her hand and drew her after him.

'No,' she shrieked. 'Gil, I haven't got anything on my feet.'

Instantly he picked her up in his arms and swung her round until she was giddy. 'Over there is where the spectators will be, behind a rope,' he said, stopping so that they faced the tents. 'Then there'll be forty yards of clear ground, before another rope. That space is the safety area, and it'll be left empty.

'Beyond that is another forty-yard strip where we'll give the display. We're standing in the middle of it now. Then there's another strip at the back which is left empty for the spent rockets to land on. We have to angle everything so that it lands there.' He kissed her robustly. 'Woman, are you prepared for a hard day's work?'

'Looks like I'm going to have to be. Do you mind if we have breakfast first?'

'You can have five minutes.'

'You're so kind.'

While she cooked Gil studied his plan of the grounds and talked. 'We start with an enormous volley of sound and brilliant colours. The more noise the better—catch their attention—get them looking up. Then, before they've got their breath, hit 'em with display rockets, display shells, golden rain. Move, Perry. Then a quieter section, and multicoloured rockets for the finale, complete with thunder effect. Perry, *move*.'

The dog moved, but only a couple of inches, to where he could beg for titbits of bacon. They ate hungrily. Now and then Gil would scribble notes, as further inspiration came to him, and when the meal was over he had a full page. 'Just a few last-minute changes,' he said, using a phrase that was to come to have an ominous ring to Jane. For, as she soon learned, 'Just a few last-minute changes' could mean anything from a couple of extra rockets to rearranging the entire show at ten minutes' notice.

The morning that followed was the toughest she'd ever known. Three young men arrived from the council and began erecting a scaffold to Gil's directions. As yesterday, his natural authority asserted itself as he insisted on being obeyed down to the smallest detail. Those who tried to cut corners were quietly but firmly told to do it again.

'He doesn't let you get away with anything, does he?' one of them observed resentfully. 'I feel sorry for you, miss. Does he order you about too?'

'Oh, me,' Jane said with a sigh. 'He's forgotten I'm here.'

She was soon to regret her words when Gil gave her the job of going over the field digging small holes from which the shells were to be fired. 'They should be at least six inches deep by three inches wide,' he told her. 'And they must be angled facing away from the spectators.'

She did her best but when Gil inspected her efforts he merely said critically, 'Too wide.'

'It's three inches,' she declared indignantly.

'More like four.'

'Well—three—four—as long as it's wide enough.'

'No, that's no good. Too wide is as bad as not wide enough. The mortar tube should fit into it snugly, not slop around, in case the shell goes off in the wrong direction. Fill it in and start again a few inches further along.'

'Yes, *sir*!'

'Oh, and by the way, the grass is a bit long here. You'd better cut it back wherever you want to dig a hole.'

'Anything else?'

He grinned and kissed the end of her nose. 'If I think of anything else I'll let you know,' he said provocatively. The next moment he'd turned away and apparently forgotten her.

Jane borrowed a pair of shears from one of the workmen, and began to snip, reflecting that whatever she'd come on this trip for it wasn't this. To add to her frustration Perry, attracted by the noise of the shears, persisted in trying to join in, so that she had to keep stopping for fear of catching his ears.

'Move, you silly dog,' she eventually told him crossly. He sloped off, the picture of forlorn rejection, but was back in seconds. Jane snipped and dug until she was sure she'd got it right, then summoned Gil to approve her efforts.

'Width perfect, angle perfect,' he declared.

'But?' she asked.

'Not deep enough.'

'Not deep enough,' she muttered rebelliously as Gil departed. 'Not deep enough. Why don't we dig a really deep hole, Perry, and bury him in it? Then see what he says. On second thoughts he'd say, "You've got the angle wrong." Why did I bother to come at all? Moonlight, roses and romance! Huh! Sarah thought I was going to have such sweet memories. I'll have memories all right—memories of an aching back, and a man who turned into Genghis Khan before my eyes. Yes, Gil, no, Gil, three bags full, Gil. *Move, dog!*'

After the digging came the filling. Each hole had a small plastic bag set into it, and into this was pushed the cardboard mortar tube that contained the shell. The plastic prevented the tube becoming soggy in the soil. By the time Jane had done twenty of these she was feeling rebellious again.

At the same time, however, she had to respect Gil's obsession with safety. He kept the key to the box of shells in his own pocket, refused to open it until the last minute, and showed her how to light them, making her repeat the actions until she'd got the safety rules firmly in her head.

'Never lean over the shell while you're lighting it,' he said again and again. 'Do it at arm's length. If it doesn't ignite at once, back off. Don't peer in to see what's happening, whatever you do, because that's when it *will* go off. Have you got that clear?'

'Of course I have,' she said, frazzled. 'When someone tells me something ten times over, I understand it. I'm bright that way.'

He grinned. 'I'm a bit of a bear today, aren't I?'

'Yes,' she said, not mincing matters. Then her sense of justice made her add, 'But I do understand.'

'Safety's important,' he said. 'I don't want to see you putting your life or your sight at risk. Now, let's get on with the work.'

He kissed her briefly, but she had the feeling that his mind was already on other things. As he walked away she wondered how she could ever have thought he was irresponsible.

At last Gil declared himself satisfied. 'Now for supper,' he said. 'I think it should be a big one, to brace us for the work ahead.'

'Then why don't we go to the steak house I passed last night?' Jane suggested, with visions of a romantic meal for two coming back into focus.

But Gil shook his head. 'I don't want to leave all this,' he said, indicating the set-up. 'You never know who might think it funny to tamper with it. I'll buy some steaks and we'll eat them outside, where I can keep my eye on things. Don't you think that's the best idea?'

'Wonderful,' Jane agreed in a colourless voice.

But she had to admit that he was right when some local lads crawled through the safety ropes and advanced on the scaffolding. Gil got rid of them firmly, and ate the rest of his meal with his eyes turned on the field. He rejected the wine Jane would have poured for him in favour of mineral water.

'I never drink before a performance,' he explained. The next moment his disarming grin appeared. 'Sorry. That sounded really pompous, didn't it? But it matters so much.'

'And I thought you were just a joker,' she said, with a mockery that was chiefly directed at herself.

'I am about most things, but not about this. This is deadly serious. I have to succeed. I *have* to...'

Jane saw that his eyes were fixed on some distant horizon, and he seemed to have forgotten about her.

'Gil?'

He returned to earth. 'I'll just give everything one more check,' he said. He took up the torch, for by now it was nearly dark, and departed on his rounds. Jane was left staring after him, astonished by what she'd briefly glimpsed. She knew by now that Gil had an artist's passion and a craftsman's efficiency, but she'd seen something else in his eyes: a driving purpose that had shaken her with its intensity.

At last darkness fell, and it was time for the show to begin. Jane was nervous, eager to do well. It wasn't their first show together, but it was the first for which her contribution had been planned. She couldn't bear the thought of letting him down.

The announcement came over the loudspeaker and the crowd began to drift towards them. Gil positioned himself at the far end, leaving Jane to work the stereo system. In the darkness all she could see was his torch. At last he clicked it on and off twice, the signal for her to start the music.

As the first notes of Handel's 'Fireworks Music' pealed out Gil went for a switch. Jane dashed into position, ready to set off the next batch of shells when the first was nearly over. She timed it beautifully, sending showers of colour up into the sky at just the right moment, and was rewarded by a brief, 'Well done,' from Gil as they raced past each other.

More shells, rockets, explosions overhead. Once she lost her place and became confused, but Gil grabbed her arm and pointed, shouting, 'There!' and she was back on course again.

Ten minutes to go. Five. She was exhilarated. She wanted this to last for ever. The cacophony was deafening as the finale began. The rockets went up, one, two, three, each explosion triggering others in a seemingly endless train.

The last shell shimmered and went out. The crowd gave a long 'Ah-h-h!' of satisfaction, followed by applause. The show was over, and people began to drift away.

'We did it!' Gil exulted. 'Our first full show together.'

'Was it a success?' she asked eagerly.

'A great success. You were wonderful.' He drew her towards him and tightened his arms to kiss her. Jane's head swam as she realised that her moment had finally come. His lips were warm and firm, and they filled her with delight. Despite her tiredness her body responded gladly. She loved him so much, wanted him so completely.

Gil drew back and gave a little sigh. 'Ah, well! Time to get to work.'

The beautiful dream vanished. Jane opened her eyes. 'Work?' she echoed, aghast. 'What else have we been doing all day?'

'We have to go over the site looking for fireworks that haven't ignited. There are always a few.'

'Do we have to do it now?' she cried.

' 'Fraid so.'

'But it's dark.'

'We use torches.' He climbed into the caravan and emerged a moment later with two buckets, filled with water. 'If you find anything, pick it up carefully and drop it in water,' he said. 'Here's your torch.'

It was half an hour before he said, 'All right, I think we've got them all. Let's pack up for the night.'

He released Perry from the caravan, where he'd been shut in for his own safety, and took him for a walk while Jane started cooking supper. While she worked she prepared a speech that she felt should be delivered as soon as possible. There were things that had to be got straight.

'Gil, I think it's time we talked about what I'm doing here—' Not quite right. 'I didn't come on this trip just to be your Girl Friday. I came because I love you, but I might as well have stayed at home.' That was how she felt, but she rejected it as too aggressive. Besides, she was wary of saying she loved him when she was no longer sure how he felt about her.

She wondered if he regretted inviting her along, but felt unable to back out. Did his free spirit flinch from their cramped living arrangements? Too close? Too like marriage? Was he compensating by keeping her at arm's length?

Gil returned rather late and breathless. 'Blame him,' he said, pointing at Perry. 'He's got a severe attack of one-year-itis.'

'One year—what?'

'He's a year old. The sap is rising, and a hot-blooded young dog starts to realise there's more to life than chasing cats. She was a very pretty poodle, but she wasn't interested.' He addressed Perry, who was looking innocent. 'You villain. When a lady says no, she means no. Is the meal ready?'

'Yes,' Jane said.

It occurred to Jane that to be talking about any form of love might give her the chance she needed, so as they ate she brought the conversation back to Perry's amorous exploits. Gil chuckled as he related the story.

'He started a very determined courtship that got him nowhere. The lady is called Fifi la Luna, according to his owner.'

'You got friendly, then?'

'I made friends with her to ward off a suit for damages. Not that Fifi needed much protecting. She's half Perry's size, but she bit him hard enough to make his eyes water. You'll be more careful who you flirt with next time, won't you, old son?'

'If he's in love, he probably won't,' Jane observed, filling Gil's glass with wine. 'Who cares for care, when love is everything?'

Gil gave his wicked grin. 'I don't think it was love so much as the canine equivalent of slap and tickle. Except that he was the one who got slapped...'

It was hopeless. Gil had gone into clowning mode and Jane wouldn't be able to get through to him now. Of course, he didn't *want* to let her through to him. His humour was just a way of keeping an emotional distance between them.

She forced herself to laugh at his droll description of Perry's disastrous courtship, but she didn't feel much like laughing. They did the dishes together and she made up the beds while he settled Perry under the caravan. By the time he returned Jane had decided that now or never was the time for her speech. She waited until he was in bed and the light was out.

'Gil—'

'Uh-huh!'

'Don't you think—? That is—there's something I've been wanting to say. Before we started this trip—I know we didn't really know each other very well but—it seemed to me— Gil? *Gil?*'

He was asleep.

CHAPTER SEVEN

Two nights later the final show was a triumph. By now Jane was getting good at setting fireworks in position, and she could shin up the scaffolding like a monkey. Everything went perfectly, and when the last light had died out of the sky the crowd cheered and clapped loudly.

Then there was the job of crawling over the field looking for unexploded shells, even more important tonight, as they wouldn't be here to do an extra check in the morning. It was a boring chore at the best of times, but it was worse now because of the muggy weather. It had been sultry all day, and the very air felt clammy. Jane was dressed in shorts and a skimpy top, to get as much air on her body as possible. She wished that decency didn't make it impossible for her to remove more. Gil was luckier. He too was in shorts, but he could tear off his vest and work bare-chested.

'There's a storm brewing,' Gil said. 'We're lucky it's held off this long. Well, I think we've found everything there is to find.'

'I'm worn out,' Jane gasped. 'Can't we stay here tonight, until the storm's passed?'

''Fraid not. We have to be off this ground by midnight. Something to do with the council's insurance. Never mind. After this we have a break. Our next venue is at the seaside, but it's not until Saturday, so we can go slowly and enjoy a couple of days by the sea.'

'Lovely,' Jane said.

That was it, she thought. Moonlight over the sea, long, romantic walks along the sand, and no work to distract Gil's attention. The mood would be perfect.

When they were almost ready to go they discovered that Perry had vanished again. 'You know what he's doing, don't you?' Gil said with a groan. 'Wolfing down scraps from the sausage stall while the world and his wife say, "Poor doggy, why don't his owners feed him properly?"' He went off towards the tents. Some of them were already down, others were being dismantled with difficulty owing to the high wind that had sprung up. Jane yawned and closed her eyes, thinking blissfully of the days to come.

'Excuse me.'

Jane opened her eyes to see a thin, middle-aged man with an anxious expression.

'My name's David Shaw,' he said. 'I enjoyed your show very much. One of the best I've seen.'

'Thank you. I'll tell Mr Wakeham.'

'Is he—is he very expensive?'

'No, he's moderate as fireworks go. Did you want a large display?'

'Oh, no. It's my little girl—her birthday party. She's ten. We were going to have a conjuror, but he's let us down at the last minute and she's so disappointed. But she loves fireworks, and it would really make it up to her.'

Smiling, Jane fished out Gil's tariff and showed it to the man. His face brightened.

'I could afford that,' he said, pointing to a display at the cheaper end. 'Oh, this is marvellous.'

Gil appeared with Perry. Mr Shaw repeated his congratulations, and Jane explained what he wanted. Gil went into a detailed explanation of how the display would look, with Mr Shaw nodding eagerly.

'That's just what I want,' he said. 'The only problem is it's tomorrow night. I know it's rather short notice, but could you do it? It would mean so much to my little girl.'

'Of course we'll do it,' Gil assured him. 'We're free until Saturday. Where are you?'

Mr Shaw gave him the address. 'It's a farm, about twenty miles from here.' He scribbled a map. 'This will show you how to get there tonight and you can park near the house. I'd show you the way, but I have to stay and see someone.' He looked up as a drop of water landed on him. 'You'd better get there quickly. It looks like a storm.'

When he'd gone Gil gave a jubilant yell. 'Another booking. Isn't that great?'

'Great,' Jane said, seeing her vision of a few perfect days by the sea vanish.

'You don't sound very pleased.'

'Of course I'm pleased for you. It's just that I was looking forward to the sea.'

'We'll have plenty of time for that. And you know the best thing of all?'

'No, tell me what's the best thing,' she said, trying to sound cheerful.

'The money. I still owe money to my suppliers, and I've got to send them most of what I made tonight. The rest will go on petrol. But with this extra booking I can repay some of your loan. Isn't that wonderful?'

'Well, I wasn't actually worried about it,' she said with a fixed smile. Inside her a voice was saying, Blow the money! Tell me you're disappointed to lose the time alone with me. But you're not, are you?

'That's sweet of you,' Gil said. 'But I was worried about it.'

'Gil,' she said, with a touch of desperation, 'there are more things in life than money!'

'That I should live to hear a bank manager belittle money!'

Jane stared. She'd forgotten she was a bank manager. 'All I meant—I was just trying to say—that I was looking forward to a few days off—together.'

'So was I. But we'll still have them, minus one day.'

'Unless another customer appears with another booking,' she said crossly.

'The more bookings, the sooner I can pay you back. I get work by word of mouth. I thought you understood.'

'Oh, yes, I understand,' she said. 'I'm beginning to understand a lot of things.'

'What's that supposed to mean?'

'Nothing. Please forget it.'

'How can I forget it when you make mysterious comments like that?'

Jane had a horrible feeling that she was being childish, but tiredness and disappointment were playing havoc with her mood. She made a huge effort and pulled herself together.

'It's nothing,' she said calmly. 'It's been a long day and we're both tired. Let's get moving. The sooner we're there, the sooner we can get something to eat.'

'But I just don't understand you.'

'No, you don't, do you?' she said, feeling her temper slipping away from her again.

'No, I don't. What's this all about?'

'Nothing.'

'Well, what have I done?'

'You haven't done anything,' she said with perfect truth.

'Then why am I in trouble?'

'Gil, are we going to get this caravan moving or are we going to stay here all night arguing?'

'I'm quite prepared to stay here all night arguing.'

'What about the council's insurance?'

'To hell with the council's insurance! What have I done to offend you?' He had to raise his voice against the wind.

'Are you going to be leaving soon, sir?' A man was coming towards them, waving a sheaf of official-looking papers. 'Everyone away before midnight. That's the rule.'

'Yes, we're going now,' Gil said. He cast Jane an infuriated glance and got into the car. A few minutes later they were on the road. 'Have you got the map Mr Shaw drew for us?' he asked.

Jane squinted at the paper. 'Yes, but I can only read when you go under a streetlamp.'

'Sorry about that,' he said irritably.

'No need to be.'

'It's hardly my fault the streetlamps are so far apart.'

'I didn't mean that. I just meant that I'm having practical difficulties.'

'Can you give me some directions, please? Which turn do I take now?'

'If that's Clayborn Road you turn left.'

'Suppose it isn't Clayborn Road?'

'I don't know,' she said crossly.

'Well, I've turned left now, so let's hope it was.'

After that it rapidly got worse. From a squabble it developed into a spat, and from there it became a full-scale row. To the outside world it might have seemed a fuss about nothing, but Jane knew she had right on her side. She was tired, hungry, disappointed, and fully entitled to be in a temper. It was equally clear that Gil was just being difficult for the sake of it. 'I didn't know you could behave like this,' she seethed at last.

He wasted no time asking what she meant. 'Everybody can behave like this,' he said reasonably. 'Everybody *does* from time to time. We just haven't seen this side of each other before. Now you're seeing mine and I'm seeing yours.'

'Mine? What do you mean, mine? I'm reason personified.'

'Ho-ho-ho!' he scoffed.

'Don't "ho-ho" me!' she said, incensed. Her temper rose to boiling point. 'Don't you sit there ho-hoing like some demented Father Christmas.'

'If I was Father Christmas and you were an elf I'd sack you,' he growled.

'Well, I'm not an elf.'

'Which way do I turn here?'

'Where?'

'Never mind, we've missed it now.'

'Sorry.'

'It might have been the turning we need.'

'I said I'm sorry,' Jane snapped.

'Some elf!'

'I'm not an elf.'

'If Santa has elves like you working for him it's a wonder he ever delivers any presents.'

'Gil, for the last time, *I am not an elf*.'

The drizzle of rain had rapidly increased. Now it turned into a downpour that had Gil's wipers working overtime. He strained to see out of the windscreen while Jane fought to make some sense of the awkwardly scribbled map.

'There should be a turning to Corydale soon,' Gil said, adding provocatively, 'Unless of course we've missed it.'

'There's a sign just up ahead. Don't drive past it too fast.'

'I'm not driving too fast. How can I in this rain?'

'I didn't say you were driving too fast,' Jane said with saintly patience. 'I merely said don't drive too fast for me to see the sign. We're nearly on it.'

Gil stopped. 'Is that slow enough for you?' he asked through gritted teeth.

'Perfectly, thank you,' she said crisply.

But the downpour obscured the letters and reluctantly she had to get out to read the sign. The rain lashed her bare legs and midriff and soaked through the skimpy top. She climbed back into the car, wet and dismal. 'Turn right for Corydale. You see, we hadn't missed the turning.'

'Good elf!' Gil was unwise enough to say.

'Gil, if you call me an elf again I swear I'll get out of this car and walk back to Wellhampton.'

'For Pete's sake! Where's your sense of humour?'

'Taking early retirement. It's been in failing health ever since this trip started.'

'Yes, I noticed. I can't think why, but suddenly you seem like a different person.'

'Ditto.'

'Me?' Gil's voice was full of outraged innocence. 'I've been trying to keep up with *your* moods, and it hasn't been easy, let me tell you.'

The sheer injustice of this held her speechless for a few moments. '*I* have been sweetness and light,' she said at last in a dangerous voice. 'I've taken everything you can throw at me—shells, rockets, dig the hole this way, that way, deeper, not so deep. I've put up with that idiot dog scratching himself whenever I'm trying to get to sleep. I've even put up with him trying to drag the caravan away when a cat passed in the night.'

'You made that up.'

'I never did. It happened last night.'

'Then why don't I remember it?'

'Because you were dead to the world,' she said bitterly. 'An earthquake couldn't have penetrated your snoring.'

'I don't snore,' he said, stung.

'Don't you ever! I've heard quieter thunderstorms.'

'I do not—may you be forgiven, woman! *I do not snore!*'

'Huh!'

'And what's "Huh!" supposed to mean?'

'It means, Huh!'

Sulphurous silence reigned for the next few miles. The rain was coming down harder than ever and all Gil's attention was taken up by trying to see ahead.

'Where have all the lights gone?' he demanded at last. 'It's pitch-dark ahead.'

'That's because we're out in the country. We should be getting near the farm soon.'

'I'd better slow down. The road's not too good.'

They lurched in and out of a pothole as he spoke. Jane hung onto the sides of her seat, while Perry was bounced six inches into the air, and looked reproachful. From far back in the caravan came the sound of a crash.

'There's the farm,' Jane said at last. Her sharp eyes had caught a glimpse of the farm sign in the headlamps. 'Turn in, quickly.'

Gil turned, and in the distance they could both make out the lights of a house. 'Where to now?' he demanded. 'The road's vanished.'

'Then I'll get out and find it for you,' Jane informed him glacially, opening the car door.

She stepped straight into a puddle. She decided to be philosophical about it. After all, what difference did it make in this downpour? Edging her way forward, she discovered another puddle, then another. Here and there were traces of what might have been a rough track. She waved to Gil and he began to follow her slowly, the caravan bouncing around behind him.

Suddenly she stopped, realising that the lights of the house had vanished. At that moment there was a flash of lightning that lit up the whole countryside, revealing fields in all directions, stretching into the darkness.

'What's up?' Gil yelled, getting out. 'Why have you stopped?'

A bellow of thunder drowned her answer. When it was over she yelled, 'I don't know where we are.'

'You said we'd reached the farm.'

'We have, but the road seems to have run out. We're just in the middle of—I don't know.'

Gil took the torch and aimed it at the ground. 'We're in the middle of a field,' he groaned. 'And this rain has turned it into a bog. Quick, we must get moving while we can.'

They jumped back into the car and Gil put his foot down frantically, but it was already too late. The caravan was settling deep into the soft earth, and the wheels merely spun in the mud.

'Damn!' he said, slamming his hand against the steering wheel in frustration. 'Here, you drive. I'll push.'

'You can't push that heavy weight,' Jane protested.

'Thank you for implying that I'm a seven-stone weakling—'

'I never—'

'Jane, get in the driving seat.'

'But—'

'Just *do it.*'

He got out and went to the back of the caravan. Jane got behind the wheel and tried to drive on, but there was no movement at all. After ten frustrating minutes she got out and went to join him.

'I'll push too,' she shouted over the rain.

'Who's driving the car? Perry?'

'Nobody's driving the car,' Jane told him with dangerous patience, 'because nobody needs to. The car isn't moving. So let's get to work.'

They set their shoulders to the caravan and heaved with all their might, but it merely settled deeper, while they slipped and slid and slithered, and Perry danced about them, yodelling with glee at finding humans who knew how to enjoy mud.

They finished up flat on the ground, exhausted and having achieved nothing. Painfully they hauled themselves into sitting positions, and sat there, breathing hard.

'So now what do we do?' Jane gasped. She was wet through, covered in mud and aching all over.

'I don't know,' Gil said. He reached out and helped her to her feet. 'We can't go forward and we can't go back. You seem to have led us right into a field.'

'I—? *I led—?*'

'Well, you were navigating. I just followed you. Look, it doesn't matter now.'

'Oh, great. You make your accusations and then you say it doesn't matter.'

'I wasn't accusing you. We're both tired—'

'But I was the one who led us into a field, right?' she demanded, incensed.

'Well, you were,' he pointed out reasonably.

'Well, *I* wasn't the one who accepted a tomfool booking at the last minute that left us trying to find a farm at the back of beyond in pitch-darkness and a storm. That may, just possibly, have played some part in our predicament.'

Another flash of lightning revealed him, standing there with rain pouring down his bare chest, which was rising and falling heavily. He was staring at her in amazement. 'So now it's my fault because I took a booking?' he demanded.

'I was looking forward to a few days off and—and we could have spent some time together. I thought that was what you wanted. I didn't know I was invited on this trip to be a drayhorse.'

'A what?'

'I'm just cheap labour, aren't I? I thought you wanted to be with me—'

'I do—'

'Oh, no, you don't. All you wanted was someone to order around. Anybody would have done.'

Gil tried to brush the sodden hair back out of his eyes. 'That's not true. I wanted *you*.'

'It looks like it, doesn't it? You've taken more notice of that dog than you have of me. A couple of patronising kisses and I'm supposed to be satisfied.'

'What do you mean, patronising?'

'You know perfectly well what I mean.'

Gil gritted his teeth. 'My kisses are not patronising.'

'They are when they're all I get. I came because I love you. I thought it was going to be a romantic trip. I thought you *wanted* me. But if I'd known how you were going to keep your distance I'd have stayed at home.'

'So now it's my fault for treating you like a lady?' Gil demanded in outrage. 'Just because I didn't pounce on you the first night—'

'Or the second, or the third—'

'Just because I didn't pounce on you like a sex-starved adolescent! I thought you deserved better than that. I was going to let you set the pace, work up to it gradually, because I respect you. I've been waiting for your signal, and all I've got is crabby criticisms.'

'If I'm crabby, whose fault is it?'

'Mine, I gather.' Gil tore at his hair. 'You idiotic woman. I'm in love with you. I have been from the start.'

'Pull the other one,' she yelled back.

She thought he muttered, 'No, it's quicker this way,' but she couldn't be sure because in the same instant he yanked her into his arms for the fiercest kiss he'd ever given her. 'I've been wanting to do this all week,' he said against her mouth, 'but you were so stand-offish—'

'Me?'

'I thought you'd come to me—'

'I thought you didn't want me—'

'Well, you know better now,' he growled, crushing her against him. Jane flung her arms around him and kissed him back with all her heart. It wasn't how she'd planned it, but she was wiser now, and knew that love happened when it happened. Despite the mud and the cold rain she was burning up with desire. She ran her hands over his bare chest, and their sodden bodies clung together in eager anticipation.

'Now do you believe me?' he demanded in a muffled voice.

'Yes—yes—kiss me—'

He did so, his mouth teasing her while his hands caressed her. The violent elements were forgotten. The only storm was the storm in their hearts.

Suddenly all the world seemed to explode with light. Through the driving rain they could hear a voice calling, 'Hey, there!'

Reluctantly Jane tore herself away from paradise to realise that, while they'd been oblivious, a sturdy vehicle had closed on them, bathing them in its headlights. A woman jumped out and made her way carefully over the soggy ground.

'I'm Celia Shaw,' she shouted. 'My husband called to say you were coming and I thought you might need a bit of help. My goodness! You *do*, don't you?' She surveyed the trapped vehicle. 'Throw some clothes into a bag and I'll take you home. We'll send a tractor to get this lot out of the mud in the morning.' She looked closely at Jane. 'Hello, there! Are you all right?'

'Yes,' Jane said vaguely. 'Yes, I'm fine.' She knew that in another moment she would have made love with Gil without caring where they were. Prim, proper Jane Landers wanted this man so much that she minded nothing, if only he could be hers. She was dazed with shock at the interruption, but her heart was still singing. He loved her. He wanted her. She knew it now. All was well with the world.

They seized some clothes from inside, and piled into Celia's car. When they'd gone a short way the lights from the house came into view again. 'They just disappeared without warning,' Jane said. 'That's why we got lost.'

'It's the trees that cover them just there,' Celia said. 'You poor things. You must be frozen.'

They should have been, sitting there in skimpy clothes, soaked to the skin. But as Jane felt Gil's hand curl around hers she felt a fierce warmth surge up inside her. When she met his eyes and saw their piercing gleam, her blood began to throb expectantly in her veins. Every inch of her body yearned for him, and soon he was going to be hers.

In a few minutes they'd reached the farmhouse, a big, rambling building, with lights pouring from the windows. Celia Shaw took them in the back way into an old-fashioned kitchen with a flagstone floor, scattered with rag rugs. It was deliciously warm, and Perry wasted no time dispossessing a black and white sheepdog and settling himself.

'There are two bathrooms,' Celia said. 'One upstairs, one down. Take one each, and by the time you're warm and dry supper will be on the table.'

Jane got thankfully under the shower and let the water wash the mud from her body. When she'd finished she noticed herself in the mirror. Her eyes were shining and eager with happiness.

She found Gil already downstairs, tucking into a large supper, while Perry tucked into an even larger one at his feet. Celia pulled out a chair for her and began to ladle food onto her plate. It was a delicious stew, and Jane ate it gladly. By the time she'd finished David Shaw had arrived home, full of apologies.

'All's well that ends well,' Gil said. He was speaking to David but his eyes were on Jane.

'I couldn't eat another thing,' she said at last.

'Can you not finish the rest?' Celia asked. 'Well, never mind. I know someone who'll like it.' She dropped the scraps onto Perry's plate, where they vanished. 'If you'll forgive my asking, are you sure you're feeding that poor creature enough?'

She showed them upstairs, to a room at the end of a long corridor. It had a low ceiling with oak beams, and a large double bed covered in a patchwork quilt.

'Goodnight now,' she said.

'Goodnight,' David called from just behind her.

Celia closed the door and returned along the passage, David hurrying after her.

'Hey,' he said. 'There's only a double bed in there. Suppose they wanted two single ones?'

'They don't.'

'How do you know?'

Celia chuckled. 'Because when I went to fetch them I saw them before they saw me.'

'Yes, but are you sure that they—?'

'*Quite* sure.'

CHAPTER EIGHT

JANE lay back across the huge bed and waited for her miracle. It came slowly. Gil lay beside her, propped up on one elbow, watching her with adoration in his eyes.

He'd undressed her with loving care, just as she'd dreamed would happen that first night. But this was infinitely more precious. Now they'd quarrelled and made up, and knew each other a thousand times better.

He touched her face softly, letting his fingers drift down her cheek and her long neck, coming to rest over the swell of her breast.

'I love you,' he said quietly.

She whispered, 'I love you,' holding out her arms to him in welcome. He came into them at once, gathering her against his heart for a long moment.

At first the pleasure was light, a soft, lingering awareness of him caressing her everywhere. His eyes were gentle and loving. His hands touched her with reverence. His kiss was an act of adoration.

Deep in her consciousness the fireworks started, luminous flames that awed her with their beauty, wheels that spun, faster and faster, throwing out darts of light. Then the rockets started, streaming up into the sky, leaving long trails of glittering light that shimmered into nothing, before starting again. She cried out with wonder, reaching her arms up to heaven. Then came the explosions of colour, red, blue, green, one after another, faster and faster. At the moment when she became entirely his the colours united into a searing white light that filled and possessed her.

And then it was gone. Heaven was dark again and she was falling to earth. But there were loving arms to catch her and hold her close, and a beloved voice whispering in her ear, 'My love...my love...'

Afterwards they lay curled blissfully in each other's arms. Jane was about to doze off when she felt Gil's body shake with laughter. 'What?' she asked.

'I thought I was being so subtle, waiting for the right time,' he said. 'I wanted to show you I knew how to behave like a gentleman.'

She joined in his laughter. 'And I was cursing you. I thought you weren't interested in me as a woman.'

'You couldn't really have believed that.'

'Oh, yes, I did. I thought I knew exactly what the first evening would be like. We'd have a romantic, candle-lit meal, and you'd give me red roses.' Indignation tinged her voice. 'After all, you gave Sarah red roses.'

He laughed tenderly at her. 'One day I'll give you a red rose. Just one. It will be perfect, and it'll come to you in an unexpected way.'

'Mm, I love mysteries. Tell me more.'

'Then it wouldn't be a mystery,' he teased.

'But I want to know.'

His lips tickled her ear. 'Nope.'

'But—Gil, if you keep doing that—'

'Yes?' he murmured, redoubling his efforts. 'Then what?'

'Then—then...' She threw her arms about him and words faded away.

Next morning David sent his tractor to rescue the caravan and bring it up to the house. The sun had come out, drying the countryside, and by the time of the party the boggy conditions had become a memory.

The show was a triumph. The children gasped and clapped like mad. David's daughter bestowed the final accolade, declaring that this was *much* better than a conjuror. Gil and Jane spent another night with the Shaws, and set off early next morning.

At the seaside a kindly farmer let them park on his land, by a stream. There was a funfair by the beach, and they went to it in memory of their first night. They bought toffee apples and funny hats, won fluffy toys, made idiotic puns and collapsed with laughter. Gil insisted on paying for a go on a stall that had plastic ducks floating in a circle. He hooked three that had the same number, and the stall holder bellowed that he'd won a prize. It turned out to be a choice from the cheapest items.

'Not another toy,' Jane begged. 'We've already got a rabbit, a gorilla, a lamb, a snake, and something that's so shapeless I don't know what it is.'

'All right, I'll have that.' Gil pointed to a small card with a ring stuck to it. It was gilt-painted plastic, with a piece of blue glass where the jewel should be. Solemnly he took her left hand and slipped the ring onto her engagement finger. 'And to think you doubted my intentions,' he declared.

Then, before she could read his face to know what he really meant, he said, 'Now come on and let's get some of that violent green liquid that every child in the place seems to be drinking.'

They drank violent green liquid and ate candy floss. Finally they went home and made love joyfully, while Perry shredded the fluffy toys all over the floor.

Next day they stayed where they were, picnicking by the stream. Gil leaned back against a tree, letting the hot sun play over his bare chest. Jane lay on the ground, her head against his leg, blissfully content.

'To think this might never have happened,' she murmured.

'It was bound to happen. I had a booking.'

'Not the booking. Us. Finding each other.'

'You mean the day I walked into the bank?'

'No.' She swatted him with a blade of grass. 'You're not usually so slow on the uptake. I mean having that row, and coming to understand each other.'

'We'd have understood each other in the end.'

'When, I wonder? After we'd reached the point of throwing dishes? No, it was David Shaw who did it, turning up unexpectedly like that.'

'Yes, but if he hadn't turned up we'd have rowed about something else, and we'd still be where we are now,' he objected logically.

'Don't spoil it,' Jane pleaded. 'You're the one who's supposed to believe in the joys of the unexpected.'

'And you're the one who's supposed to believe in common sense.'

'Oh, hang common sense! Who needs it when life is glorious?'

'Does this way of life really suit you, Jane?'

She yawned and stretched. 'It's the only way to live. Oh, I wish we could go on like this for ever.'

'Living hand to mouth? Never knowing where the next job is coming from?'

'You'll always get work because you're brilliant,' she said contentedly.

'Bless you. You know how to say the right thing.'

They lay still, in drowsy contentment, for a while. At last she murmured, 'I don't know myself any more. Usually I have to be getting on with something all the time, but now all I want to do is laze here with you. It's as though I'm turning into a completely different person.'

'Not different,' he said. 'Just another side of you. It's been there all the time, waiting for its chance.'

'But it's so different to my usual self, it's like sharing my body with a stranger.'

'That's the best way,' he murmured. 'To start again—make yourself over and be someone else...'

Jane stared up at him. Gil's voice had a new note of seriousness, and he was gazing into the distance, except that the distance seemed to be inside himself.

'You sound as if you really mean that,' she said curiously.

He looked at her with sudden intentness. 'Would you love me whoever I was—I mean, whatever kind of person I was inside?'

'But I love you because you're you,' she said, puzzled.

'But who am I?'

'Gil Wakeham.'

'No, no, that's just a name, nothing but a jumble of sounds. I could just as easily be called Horace Sproggins. But *me*—inside—where it matters—'

'That's the man I love,' Jane said. 'Inside, where it matters.'

He seemed to relax. 'I'll remind you one day that you said that.'

She gave him an impish grin. 'Mind you, I might have a problem if you were called Horace Sproggins.'

He laughed, and the moment passed. Jane yawned, stretched and settled back into her former contented position against him. 'Gil, why don't you get a mobile phone?' she asked sleepily. 'It makes sense with all the travelling you do.'

Unexpectedly his face set. 'No way,' he said firmly. 'If people can get you on a mobile there's no escape from the world.'

'But you don't want to escape the world,' she pointed out reasonably. 'You want the world to call you up and offer you bookings.'

'My world is here,' he said, kissing her. 'The rest of it can go hang.'

'But the fireworks...?' she murmured.

'The fireworks can go hang as well,' he said against her mouth.

For the next few minutes his kiss made everything else disappear. But when she came back down to earth Jane's practical side reasserted itself. 'What do people do if they want to contact you when you're away?' she asked thoughtfully.

'They leave a message on my answering machine and I pick it up at the next stop.'

'Answering machine? So you do have a proper home?'

'I have a place where I can be reached. This—' he indicated the caravan '—this is home. And wherever you are.'

'Mm, that's lovely, but don't you think—?'

'No,' he said firmly, lowering his mouth again. 'I don't think, on principle.'

Despite having resolved their differences they didn't find things plain sailing. When they left the seaside Gil took on another last-minute booking, which would have been worth several hundred pounds if he'd managed to get paid. But the man with the money vanished fast, leaving Gil confronting the man's bewildered staff. Since there was no time to chase him and nothing in writing they were forced to chalk it up to experience.

After the first anger Jane was inclined to shrug it off, but she soon realised that there were repercussions.

'We're running low on money and I have to buy more stock to replace the stuff I used up on that crook,' Gil told her.

'Then let me help.'

'You've done enough. You've bought most of the food and some petrol. I don't want to take any more from you.'

But when he called his suppliers to ask for an urgent delivery at the next venue he found they wanted him to pay by credit card, which he couldn't as he didn't have one. Jane saved the situation by guaranteeing payment, referring them to Kells to establish her credentials. Gil accepted the situation with good grace, but she could tell he was unhappy.

'Don't worry,' she said, trying to cheer him up. 'Something will turn up.'

'I hope it does,' he said disconsolately. 'I want to repay you fast.'

'Then we'll cross our fingers and hope for a miracle.'

That night, when Gil lay sleeping against her, she crossed the fingers of both hands and hoped with all her heart that the misfortune wouldn't be allowed to spoil this perfect time together.

'I want a real miracle,' she whispered into the darkness. 'Not the kind that comes in disguise.'

But when the miracle came it was in heavy disguise until the very last moment.

* * *

From the sea they turned inland, to Delford Manor, a fine house set in its own grounds among rolling hills, where a big wedding was to be held.

'Miss Patricia Delford is uniting herself in wedlock with Antony Ralph Hamilton-Smythe,' Gil explained.

'Smythe with a Y?' Jane asked.

'Naturally. Everything thrown in. Palatial banquet, vintage champagne, dancing and fireworks. The following morning the happy couple leave for Bermuda, courtesy of the groom's father, Brigadier Delford.'

'Do we tug our forelocks?'

'Probably. Wait and see.'

The iron gates that fronted the Delford estate seemed to indicate forelock-tugging. So did the suspicious individual who let them in and showed them where to park, well away from the big house. After half an hour an elegant, middle-aged woman appeared and introduced herself as Mrs Delford.

'The bride is my daughter,' she explained in a high-pitched, brittle voice. 'She particularly wanted fireworks for her wedding, and her father refuses her nothing. Personally I really couldn't see— However, you're here now. I suppose you've got all you want? Good.'

'No,' Gil said.

'I beg your pardon?'

'We haven't got all we want. First I'd like someone to show me the area where I'm to do the show. Then I need to collect some water.'

'I thought these things had all mod cons,' Mrs Delford said, indicating the caravan.

'It has a pipe that can be attached to a water supply, but I'm nowhere near one,' Gil explained. 'So I have to fill two large containers with water. Perhaps you can tell me where I can do that?'

His reluctant hostess looked pained. 'You can go to the back of the house,' she said. 'There's a tap on the outside wall that we use for the hose pipe.'

'Is it drinking water?' Gil asked.

'I beg your pardon?'

'Is it drinking water?' He added politely, 'We need to drink it.'

'Oh, well, I suppose you'd better go to the kitchen. Tell Cook I said it was all right.'

'Thank you,' Gil said with careful restraint.

'I'll send someone to— *Aagh!*' Mrs Delford had frozen in horror, her hand outstretched towards the caravan window, through which Perry could be seen peering curiously. 'What is that?' she demanded, aghast.

'That's a dog,' Gil said. 'He's mine.'

'You had no right to bring him here.'

'He's perfectly harmless,' Jane said indignantly. 'He doesn't chase sheep or dig up flowerbeds.' She crossed her fingers, hoping she'd just spoken the truth.

'I am a breeder of basset-hounds,' Mrs Delford said awfully.

'Well, Perry's a basset-hound,' Gil said.

'Possibly, but there are basset-hounds and basset-hounds. Mine are animals of the highest pedigree.'

'How do you know Perry doesn't have a pedigree?' Jane demanded, getting more annoyed by the minute.

Mrs Delford gave a pained smile. 'His circumstances hardly suggest it, do they? He must be kept well away from my animals *at all times*. Is that clear?'

'Perfectly,' Gil said crisply. 'I too prefer to keep my dog segregated from undesirable contacts.'

If his hostess noted any irony in his tone she ignored it. 'I'll send someone to you,' she said faintly, and turned to depart. At the last moment she stopped. 'I almost forgot. A young woman telephoned yesterday and left a message for you to call back as soon as you got here. You shouldn't really have left our number.'

'I didn't,' Gil said. 'I left her a list of my venues. She must have looked the number up.'

'Oh, you know who it is, then. Good, because I didn't catch her name. You can use the phone in the kitchen.' She departed.

'Why don't we just leave at once?' Jane seethed.

'Because I gave my word I'd be here,' Gil said. 'My word is my bond. A banker should appreciate that.'

'I don't feel like a banker. I feel like a peasant,' Jane said crossly.

'That's because you look like one,' Gil told her with a grin.

She looked down and realised that he was right. She was wearing shorts, T-shirt and sandals. Her hair was tousled and her skin tanned.

'It's amazing how people judge you by your clothes,' Gil said. 'Dress like a tramp and you'll be treated like a tramp. Dress in white tie and tails and you'll get a different reception.'

She looked at him. 'White tie and tails? You?' she said hilariously.

He gave an uncomfortable laugh. 'There's no knowing what a man may come to.' He vanished into the caravan, leaving Jane to reflect on his strange moment of uneasiness.

By the time he emerged she'd disconnected the car from the caravan and loaded the empty water containers onto it. 'Right, let's go and get that water.'

'There's no need for us both to go,' Gil said quickly. 'Why don't you start supper?'

'How can I without water? I'll come with you and drive the water back here while you're making your call.'

They found the kitchen at last. Jane filled the containers and returned alone. In a few minutes the head gardener appeared and took her to see the area that had been set aside for the show. Calling on her newly acquired experience, she told him that it was fine, and hurried back to fetch Gil to see it himself.

But there was no sign of him. It seemed the call was taking a long time. It was twenty minutes before he appeared, and even from a distance she could see that there was a shadow on his face.

'What's wrong?' she asked anxiously.

'Nothing,' he said quickly. 'There was a misunderstanding, but I sorted it out. I met the gardener on the way back. He said he'd shown you the site.'

'Yes, it's just over there. What kind of misunderstanding?'

'Nothing important. Is the site any good?'

'I thought it was fine, but you'd better see it. What was the problem?'

'I told you I sorted it out,' Gil said, with more of an edge to his voice than she'd ever heard.

'All right, don't snap at me. If there are problems I want to share them.'

He put an arm round her shoulders and hugged her. 'Sorry. You know how I get when I'm setting a show up. Come and show me where they've put us.'

He pronounced the site excellent, and praised her extravagantly for judging it so well. At any other time his praise would have thrilled her, but now she had a little nagging feeling that he was trying to distract her from his phone call. Then she pushed the thought aside. Obviously Gil had a niche in a business centre that took his calls and passed on messages. He'd as good as told her so when he'd said he had a place where he could be reached. What was there in that to worry her?

When they returned to the caravan a very pretty young woman was there, flirting with Perry through the window. 'I'm Patricia,' she said, smiling. They both liked her at once. There was a frank down-to-earthness about her that contrasted pleasantly with her mother.

'I've come to invite you to supper,' she said. 'Mummy was just devastated when she realised she'd forgotten to ask you.' In the awkward silence that followed Patricia blushed. 'Mummy doesn't mean anything by it. She sort of got carried away when Daddy became a brigadier. But we'd love to have you, honestly.'

'And Perry?' Gil asked, indicating the window with his head.

'Well, no, I'm afraid he'd have to stay here.'

'Then I think we should stay with him,' Gil said, to Jane's relief. 'You see, the three of us are a team. We stick together. Also, my partner and I have some plans to make for tomorrow. But please thank your mother for her overwhelming invitation.'

Patricia's face quivered and she just choked back a giggle. She bid them goodbye and hurried away, but half an hour later there was a knock on their door, and she was there again.

'Champers,' she said, holding out a couple of bottles. 'I pinched some from the reception. Don't tell Mum.' She was off again before they could thank her.

They spent the evening making plans for the following day, and retired early. It seemed to Jane that there was something different about Gil's lovemaking that night. He was as tender and passionate as always, but the sixth sense of love told her that part of his mind was elsewhere, worrying about something.

Later, as they lay in each other's arms, he said, 'Jane, you do love me, don't you?'

'Yes,' Jane replied.

'And trust me?'

'Of course I trust you,' she said at once.

You said that too firmly, said a voice in her mind. Why should he question it, unless...?

She managed to silence the voice at last, but when she slept it was uneasily, and she woke within an hour, feeling restless. She got quietly out of bed, pulled on some jeans and a top, and slipped out of the caravan. It was a heavenly night, lit by a brilliant moon, and she wandered at will through the gardens, enjoying their silver-touched beauty. At last she turned a corner and came unexpectedly on a small building, from which came lights. She was about to turn back when someone called, 'Who's there?'

Jane froze, recognising the voice of Mrs Delford, and before she could slip away her hostess came to the door and saw her. 'You haven't brought that dog with you?' she asked at once.

'No, I was just catching a breath of fresh air—on my own.'

'In that case you can come in. I'm having some tea.'

Jane went inside and found herself in what seemed to be a very luxurious kennel. It contained only one dog, a really beautiful basset-hound with limpid eyes, who scuttled over to the mesh of her pen and eagerly sought Jane's attention.

'Come in,' Mrs Delford said, opening the door of the pen. It was clear that she'd been sitting inside with the dog. She locked the door firmly behind Jane.

'I'm keeping her apart at the moment,' she explained. 'She was to be mated today, but there's been a delay, and they can't get here until tomorrow. It's going to make a busy day, but it can't be helped.'

'What's her name?' Jane asked, tickling the bitch's ears.

'Lady Tillingforth of Westrock,' Mrs Delford said. 'But to me she's just Tilly.' Her love for the dog had thawed her and made her a lot more likable.

She took out a Thermos flask, unscrewed two cups from the top and poured them one each. Jane settled down comfortably on the floor, and Tilly promptly snuggled up to her. Mrs Delford smiled.

'She doesn't usually take to strangers,' she said. 'She's quite highly strung, and only a year old. This will be her first litter.'

'So you're going to be a bride as well?' Jane said to Tilly. 'What's the groom like?'

'He's Lord Bertram Hannenmere of Marshall Denby,' Mrs Delford said proudly. 'Although I believe he answers to Bert.' She looked pained. 'You'd think at least they'd call him Bertie.'

'What's wrong with Bert?' Jane asked.

Mrs Delford winced. 'It's such a lower-class abbreviation.'

'And he's an upper-class dog?'

'Certainly he is.' She began to discourse on the breeding of bassets, and Jane listened contentedly. It seemed that the services of Tilly's prospective groom carried a tag of five hundred pounds.

'For that money he must be the best,' Jane said, sipping her tea.

'Well, the real best are the Moxworth bassets,' Mrs Delford conceded reluctantly. 'They've produced three Best of Breeds at Crufts. For one of them you pay a thousand. I'd gladly have paid it, but they only mate with bloodlines that already have proven champions.'

'Snobs,' Jane said at once.

'It's to protect the Moxworth reputation. Their motto is that every litter produces at least one winner, and it helps if the mother has winning genes too.'

'Poor Tilly,' Jane said, patting the bitch. 'Turned down as not good enough.'

Mrs Delford regarded her curiously. 'You speak like an educated woman. What on earth are you doing travelling the roads with that disreputable young man?'

'I'm just on holiday,' Jane said. 'I'm really a bank manager.'

The other woman didn't answer, but she raised a satirical eyebrow, and it was clear that she thought Jane was either fantasising or making fun of her. Considering the picture she'd presented all day, Jane wasn't sure she could blame her.

Mrs Delford put away the flask. 'Ah, well, I suppose I'd better go and get some sleep to nerve myself for this wedding.'

'Which one?' Jane asked impishly, and Mrs Delford's face relaxed into a smile.

'Patricia's all right,' she said. 'She's the sort of girl who can wrap men round her little finger. Always has been. It's my darling Tilly who needs looking after.' She kissed the bitch's head and led the way out of the pen, carefully locking the door.

Once outside she reverted to her other self, bid Jane a cool goodnight, and departed. Jane crept back to the caravan. Gil had just woken up.

'Where did you go?' he mumbled, drawing her back into bed.

'I went for a walk and found Mrs Delford with one of her pedigree bassets—a lovely little bitch called Tilly. It's her big day tomorrow too, and she's being kept apart, ready for her groom. Perry, get off.' The hound had pounced on her eagerly. 'What's got into you tonight?'

'Have you been cuddling Tilly?' Gil asked with a chuckle.

'Yes. Oh, heavens! Go away, Perry. And behave yourself tomorrow. This lady is an aristocrat. She's not for the likes of you.'

Eventually she persuaded him to get down, and he stretched out on the floor, heaving a mournful sigh of rejection.

CHAPTER NINE

IN THE morning, Jane surfaced out of a deep sleep, and became gradually aware that Gil was sitting beside the bed, rapidly sketching something. 'Don't move,' he said tensely.

She lay still while he finished his sketch. At last he showed it to her and she realised he'd been drawing her as she lay asleep, naked and replete with love.

'Like it?' he asked.

She chuckled. 'Did I really have that cat-that-swallowed-the-cream look on my face?'

'You looked exactly like that. Beautiful.'

She studied the sketch. Gil was a talented artist. The picture might have been called *Love Fulfilled* for its perfect depiction of a woman full of physical contentment and emotional joy. Any woman would have been honoured to have the man she loved draw her like this.

'I wish we didn't have to get up,' she said, yawning.

'Speak for yourself,' he teased her. 'I've been up for the last hour. Come on, sleepyhead. We've got a show to put on.'

He went out, leaving the sketch behind. Jane hugged it to her, wondering what on earth she'd been worrying about. The events of yesterday seemed a million years away.

It was a glorious day for a wedding. The sun beamed down on the huge marquee where the reception was to be held. Vans were already arriving with flowers and food; staff were setting up tables and sweeping gleaming white covers over them.

Jane shut Perry firmly into the caravan, ignoring his protests, and started taking boxes of shells out to the site. For the next hour she went through her usual routine of digging angled holes and filling them with mortar tubes. Gil was working on the scaffolding, assisted by the gardener.

At three o'clock in the afternoon the cars left for the church. Work redoubled to get everything finished before they returned. Two hours later the first car reappeared. The waiters came to attention. The car glided to a halt, and Patricia, a vision in frothy white, alighted.

'We'll have some supper and put our feet up until we're needed,' Gil said.

They feasted on bacon and eggs. From the tents they could hear the sounds of speeches, toasts and laughter. Jane thought that this was exactly the sort of wedding she would have had if she'd married Kenneth. But Gil? What would their wedding be like? Would there ever be a wedding? She touched the plastic ring on her left hand. Gil had never directly mentioned marriage, but he'd put the ring on her engagement finger and said his intentions were honourable.

For a moment common sense butted in, asking how she could possibly marry a man who was a fly-by-night. But, using the skills she'd developed over the last two weeks, she succeeded in dismissing common sense.

As the light faded the band struck up, and there was dancing on the lawn. Coloured lamps hung among the trees, and couples walked beneath the branches, their arms entwined.

'Shall we dance?' Gil asked, with an elegant half-bow that contrasted with his worn jeans and T-shirt. 'They won't be needing us until it's a little darker.'

They clasped each other and waltzed to the time of the music that floated to them across the lawn. Jane could see the white dress billowing as the bride danced with her groom, and she wondered if Patricia was as happy as she was herself. Everything seemed to be reaching her through a mist of happiness. As if from far away she saw a car arrive and Mrs Delford go to meet it. A man got out, bringing with him a magnificent basset-hound. He spoke to Mrs Delford, apparently making apologies.

'The groom's finally arrived,' Jane murmured.

'Eh? Oh, that groom. The one who's going to put Perry's nose out of joint. Come to think of it, we ought to give him a little walk before the show.'

'Yes, I suppose we should.'

Reluctantly Jane disengaged herself and went to the caravan. Then she froze.

'Gil, the door's open.'

'It can't be. I shut it.'

'But did you actually lock it?'

'Well, no, but—' He fell silent as the mass of scratch marks on the door told their own story. Perry had been very, very determined to escape. 'Don't panic,' he told Jane. 'You know what he's like. He'll be roving among the guests begging titbits. By now he's probably had half the wedding cake and they'll be calling us heartless monsters who let him starve.'

'Let's hope it's only that. Come on.'

They hurried to the marquee, trying to look inconspicuous. At first glance there was no sign of Perry, but the tablecloths swept the floor and might hide anything.

'Over there,' Jane said. 'There's a couple tossing food to something on the ground.'

But the something turned out to be a poodle, deeply affronted at having her supper disturbed. Jane and Gil exchanged appalled glances. People were beginning to stare at them.

'There's no help for it,' Gil muttered. 'You take that side and I'll take this side.'

As one, they ducked under the tablecloths and began to crawl along, searching and hissing Perry's name. They'd just met again in the middle when the storm broke.

Mrs Delford's wail of horror had started at a distance and reached full volume by the time she arrived at the marquee.

'Mother, whatever's the matter?' That was Patricia.

'Tilly has gone. There was a hole under the wall of the pen, and she's gone.'

'She probably got bored being alone and went into the house,' Patricia tried to soothe her.

Another voice, a man's. 'I've been down to the caravan, madam, but the two individuals appear to have vanished.'

'I knew it! They've kidnapped Tilly.'

Gil buried his head in his hands. 'Couldn't we just stay here until they've all gone home?' he pleaded.

'Come on. Let's face the music.' Jane took his hand and together they crawled out from under the table, like a pair of naughty children, she thought.

'What have you done with my Tilly?' Mrs Delford demanded in an awful voice.

'Nothing,' Jane said. 'We don't know where your Tilly is.'

'And I suppose it's just coincidence that you were hiding under the table?'

'We weren't hiding,' Gil said. 'We were looking for Perry.' In the ghastly silence that followed he said, 'He's missing too—I'm afraid.' He added quickly, 'But that might not mean anything—'

'Nonsense! Of course it means something,' Mrs Delford cried. 'Oh, my poor Tilly! *Where are they now?*'

'There,' said one of the guests, and every head turned as one. A few yards away under the lamp-hung trees, the lovers could be seen gambolling happily. Perry was nudging Tilly romantically with his nose.

'I'm afraid we're too late,' Gil said mildly.

Mrs Delford turned on them. 'You'll pay for this,' she said. 'How dare you let that mongrel loose?'

That did it. Gil drew himself up to his full height, suddenly the picture of affronted dignity. 'I'll have you know, madam,' he declared, 'that, far from being a mongrel, my dog's full name is Prince Pericles Heyroth Talleyrand of Moxworth. The *fourth*.'

'Oh, really!' Mrs Delford sneered. 'I suppose you dreamed that up last night, after your companion told you what I'd said.'

'I didn't tell him what you'd said,' Jane said quickly.

'I don't believe you, young woman.' With a sudden descent from high horse to robustness, Mrs Delford added, 'If that animal is a Moxworth, I'm the Queen of Sheba!'

'Well, Your Majesty, if you'll just wait here a moment,' Gil said smoothly, 'I'll fetch his papers.'

He marched off to the caravan, leaving Jane with the company. Patricia took pity on her and pressed a glass of champagne into her hands, but it was still the most uncomfortable few minutes she'd ever spent. Mrs Delford glared. Bert's owner looked affronted, and Bert himself gazed around in bewilderment. Jane concentrated on her champagne, wondering what would happen when Gil couldn't produce the papers.

But when he returned he had documents in his hand, which he offered to Mrs Delford. The change in that lady's features as she read them was almost comic. Jane held her breath. But Mrs Delford was made of stern stuff, and she didn't yield so easily.

'It's not the same dog,' she declared. 'It can't be.'

'Read the description of the markings, then compare them with Perry's,' Gil offered.

Perry ambled over on command, an adoring Tilly bringing up the rear. Mrs Delford examined him closely, constantly referring to the papers. All around them the wedding festivities had ground to a halt.

'It's the same dog, Mother,' Patricia said at last. 'There's no doubt about it.'

Mrs Delford raised bewildered eyes. 'But how—?'

'Does it matter?' Jane broke in. 'The point is, you've gained your heart's desire. All we have to discuss now is the price.'

'Pri—?'

'A thousand pounds, I think you said,' Jane continued. 'That's what a Moxworth bridegroom fetches. You also said something about paying it gladly. Considering what the pups will be worth you'll get it all back, and more.'

'Yes, but what about me?' Bert's owner put in. 'We agreed a fee for Bert.'

'But he hasn't earned it,' Mrs Delford pointed out swiftly.

'That's not his fault. He was willing.'

'He was late.'

'That's not his fault either. And he was *willing.*'

'Barkis was willing,' Gil murmured mischievously in Jane's ear.

'Shush!' she said, stifling a giggle.

'Sorry, Madam Bank Manager.'

'Of course Bert must have his fee,' Jane said. 'In consideration of the special circumstances, Mr Wakeham is willing to allow you a discount of fifty per cent.'

'Is that right?' Mrs Delford demanded of Gil suspiciously.

'My business manager makes my decisions,' he said, indicating Jane. 'I just do as I'm told.'

'And as a gesture of goodwill,' Jane added, 'we are willing to allow our valuable dog to spend more time with Tilly before we leave tomorrow morning.'

Mrs Delford's face was wreathed in smiles. There were cheers and laughter. Patricia presented all three hounds with pieces of wedding cake. Then somebody remembered that there was a firework display still to come. Mrs Delford hoisted Tilly into her arms, but before she left she met Jane's eyes.

'You really are a bank manager, aren't you?' she said.

'Yes,' Jane said with a smile. 'I really am.'

There had never been such a display as the one they gave that night. Gil had concentrated on white and silver fireworks, with just a few colours thrown in to avoid monotony. There was no time to discuss the evening's events. They were kept busy running hither and thither until the finale—a set piece of two hearts intertwined, which had the guests on their feet, cheering and clapping.

It was over. The party broke up. Those who were staying in the house began to drift off to bed. Arms entwined, Jane and Gil strolled down to the caravan in perfect peace and understanding.

'You're wonderful,' he said. 'All our problems solved in a moment.'

'I could have done it earlier if I'd known about Perry's ancestry. You need never go short of money again. When funds run low, you just hire him out. I'm sure he wouldn't mind.'

'He wouldn't. I would. I want to succeed through fireworks and only fireworks. I'm grateful to both of you for tonight, but it was a one-off.'

'But why only fireworks?'

'Because that's the way it is,' he said with a touch of mulishness.

Later that night, as they snuggled up, ready to go to sleep, Gil chuckled. 'You know, the really annoying thing is that that dog made more money in ten minutes enjoying himself than you and I earn in a week's hard work.'

Throughout the trip Jane kept in regular contact with Sarah. Sometimes her grandmother was in, and sometimes Jane found herself talking to the answering machine. It was clear that Sarah's social life was still prospering.

As soon as they reached the next stop Jane found a phone booth and called again. Sarah answered at once. She sounded annoyed.

'Whatever is the matter?' Jane asked.

'That insufferable man is the matter. Kenneth.'

'What's he done?'

'He came to see me, and bored on for hours about how you needed saving from yourself. I don't know how I endured it.'

'I'm sorry. I'll have a word with him.'

'Yes, he wants you to call him for "a very urgent talk", as he put it.'

'It probably isn't urgent at all.'

Sarah sounded awkward. 'Well, actually, darling, I may have been the teensiest little bit indiscreet.'

'What have you told him?' Jane asked with deep foreboding.

'About you lending Gil money.'

'Oh, Sarah, how could you? Well, never mind. There's nothing he can do, except waffle.'

After some hesitation she called Kenneth. 'Thank heavens!' he said. 'I've been out of my mind with worry, thinking of you alone with that man.'

'Kenneth, if you just want to abuse Gil then I—'

'It's more serious than that. I've been doing some checking up on your strange friend.'

'You had no right to check up on him—'

'Somebody had to act responsibly, and I could see that it wasn't going to be you. Do you know that legally Gil Wakeham doesn't exist? He isn't on any official computer—'

'You've probably been looking in the wrong place. He moves around so much that—'

'Listen, I managed to track down his suppliers. They know nothing about him either. He always pays cash. He doesn't even have a credit card. Not one. In these days.'

'You make that sound like a crime.'

'As a bank manager you know that a respectable man has paperwork, a credit account, an *address* for Pete's sake! Face facts. He's using a false name. He's probably just come out of prison.'

'I don't believe it,' Jane said furiously.

'Jane, he's a con man. Look how he's turned your head. That's how con men work. You'll be in trouble when the bank discovers that you've lent him money.'

'The bank won't know about it,' Jane said. 'It was my own money.'

'Well, that's it, then,' Kenneth retorted scornfully. 'He operates by conning money out of silly women. You'll never see a penny back. And when the money's gone you'll never see *him* again either.'

For a moment Jane hovered on the edge of losing her temper, but she controlled it. Kenneth meant well. He knew nothing about the rockets that exploded when she was in Gil's arms, and the beauty that made it impossible to believe anything against her lover.

'Please try not to worry about me,' she said. 'I know Gil better than you, and I trust him completely.'

'So you say. But what do you actually know about him?'

'I know the things that matter,' she said firmly.

'Such as where he comes from, who his family is? I don't think you know any of that. Is he married?'

'Of course not!'

'Has he told you he isn't?'

'I haven't asked him.'

'Heaven give me patience! And since he's using a false name you can't check. And what about that savage beast I saw in the back of his car? Do you trust *him?*'

Jane laughed. 'Perry isn't a savage beast. He's a pedigree basset-hound, and he's got a lovely nature.'

'Pedigree, my foot!'

'He is. His full name is Prince Pericles Heyroth Talleyrand of Moxworth, the fourth.'

Kenneth snorted. 'And what's a dubious character like Gil Wakeham doing with a pedigree dog? Stolen, most likely.'

'He's not stolen. Gil has the paperwork for him.'

'In whose name?'

'I don't know. His, I suppose.'

'Did you actually see his name on the paperwork?'

'No, but—'

'Well, there you are, then.'

'Goodbye, Kenneth,' Jane said firmly, and hung up.

She returned to find Gil cooking supper. 'All right?' he asked. 'You were a long time.'

'Yes, I'm fine. I had to call Kenneth and listen to his dire warnings about you.'

Gil grinned. 'What did he say?'

'He thinks you've just been released from prison, and that Perry is stolen.'

Gil gave a crack of laughter that almost made him drop the frying-pan. 'Do you believe him?'

'Of course not,' Jane said robustly. She considered him with her head on one side. 'I suppose you could always have *escaped* from prison.'

Gil shook his head. 'Too stupid,' he said.

'True. Still, you are a man of mystery. You never talk about your family, or anything like that.'

He kissed her. 'You know the only things about me that matter.'

'Of course I do,' she said. His words were an echo of her own to Kenneth only a short time ago. She tried to brush aside the thought that they suddenly sounded hollow.

Next day something happened that gave her another glimpse of just how little she knew about Gil. Searching in a drawer for a screwdriver, she came across a notebook in which he'd written the details of his financial transactions, including her loan. She flicked through the pages idly, noting that it was all set out with a neatness that belied Gil's carefree manner.

She was about to put the book away when she discovered something that made her pause. A year ago Gil had taken out another loan, for three thousand pounds. It had been paid off, although not always regularly. The final figure included an amount of interest that made her whistle. The sound brought Gil.

'I didn't mean to pry,' she said awkwardly. 'But I suppose that's what I'm doing.'

'It's all right. What do you think?'

'I think whoever loaned you this money ripped you off. How could you be so naïve as to go to him?'

'He was the only one who'd look at me.'

'He was a crook,' Jane yelped in outrage.

Gil laughed at her indignant face. 'Actually he's a respectable stockbroker. He's very well thought of in the City.'

'You've written "Dane" up here. I've heard of a stockbroking firm called Dane & Son.'

'It's the son.'

She stared. 'You know a stockbroker? You're friends with him?'

Gil hesitated. 'I know him. Friend is too strong a word. I don't like him.'

'I'm not surprised. He's a crook,' Jane repeated stubbornly.

'Not a crook, just a man who sees the money-making chance in everything.'

'And stockbroking isn't enough for him? He's a loan shark on the side?'

'Well, actually I'm the only one he's ever loaned money to. And he didn't want to do it even for me. He doesn't approve of me. We don't see eye to eye about what's important. He's a predator. He was brought up in the financial jungle and took to it easily. It didn't make him a very nice man, I'm afraid. Anyway, I'm out of his clutches now.'

'I should hope so. How did you come to know him at all?'

'We were at the same school,' Gil said briefly.

Now Jane felt she'd been given a clue to some of Gil's contradictions. Sarah had said he had sophisticated tastes. It looked as if his parents had been sufficiently well off to send him to an expensive school, but had suffered a crash later. That would explain a lot. She looked round, wanting to ask him more questions, but he'd gone outside and started work.

The show was more elaborate now, with all the new fireworks in place. As Gil had promised they were the best, and the crowd's reactions confirmed it. This show, he promised, would be a blockbuster. He'd spent a lot of time arranging a set piece for the end. He hadn't told Jane what it was, and she found it hard to guess from looking at it 'cold'.

With the new set-up there was twice as much work, and once they'd started she was on the go non-stop. She had no doubt now that Gil's decision to invest in new fireworks rather than a computer had been wise, but the running around left her breathless.

At last it was time for the set piece. 'Go out in front,' Gil told her. 'Tell me what it looks like.'

'Don't you need me back here?'

'No, it's more important that you see it.'

She dodged round the front just as the set piece began to light up. At first the crowd was puzzled, then as the picture became plain they began to clap and cheer. Jane watched with her mouth open and indignation in her heart.

It was a picture of a reclining woman. Gil had cunningly suggested her nakedness, without being too obvious. The whole thing was delicate and charming, but what aroused Jane's wrath was the fact that it exactly matched the drawing he'd done of her a few days ago.

'You ought to be shot, Gil Wakeham,' she told him as soon as they were alone again.

'What, for paying a tribute to you?' he asked innocently.

'Tribute, my foot!'

'But it was. You looked so beautiful lying there, I wanted the whole world to know how beautiful you were—at one remove, of course.'

She tried to maintain her annoyance, but there was no resisting the sparkle of mischief in his eyes, and at last she gave up. 'Why can't I stay mad at you?' she asked helplessly.

'Because you adore me madly, that's why,' he teased.

'Oh, do I? You're very sure of yourself.'

'Well, I've got a lot to be sure about,' he said, slipping an arm around her waist.

She went to him gladly, but before she could return his embrace they heard a voice call, 'Anyone about?'

They looked up to find a thick-set middle-aged man, with a genial expression, bearing down on them. 'Joe Stebbins,' he said, holding out a pudgy hand. 'Here's my card.'

The card proclaimed him to be an organiser of light entertainment.

'That was a good show,' he said. 'I'm setting up several things that could do with something like that. Haven't gone in for fireworks before, but great way to end an evening.' He spoke in staccato bursts.

'You mean you might have work for me?' Gil asked eagerly.

'Yes, and plenty of it. You've got something unusual. That last picture, the lady. Really original. Now look, I need to see you again before we can finalise anything, and I'm going away for a couple of weeks. Write to me at this address and let me know where you'll be. If you're as good then as you were tonight I'll have some big bookings for you. I pay good money. Ask around. Anyone'll tell you. 'Night.'

He disappeared, leaving them staring at the card.

'This is it!' Gil gasped. 'The breakthrough. If I win this I've made it. And then—' He looked at her as if trying to decide whether to say something.

'And then?' she asked hopefully.

'And then—lots of things will happen. We'll make them happen. We'll create a display together, the best we've ever done. Then we'll set it off together.'

'Together,' she murmured blissfully.

CHAPTER TEN

IT WAS late on a Thursday evening when they finally drew up outside Jane's home. 'I can't believe it's all over,' she said sadly. 'It was so marvellous.'

'Yes, it was. It'll be a week before I can be back, but I'll call you.'

'Come up and see Sarah.'

'No, give her my love. I have to be off.'

'Where to?'

'I'll tell you another time.'

Perry licked her ear, and Jane immediately embraced him. 'Goodbye, love of my life,' she murmured against his fur.

'I thought I was the love of your life,' Gil objected.

'Perry first, then you.'

'Well, we'll have to change that.' Gil firmly ejected Perry and took her into his arms. The kiss that followed drove thoughts of everything but him out of her head.

He carried her bags to the lift, kissed her briefly again, and was off. Jane stood watching him go, feeling an ache in her heart.

She'd called ahead to let Sarah know when she would be back, and her grandmother was waiting up for her.

'I don't have to ask,' she said, when she saw Jane. 'Your eyes are shining.'

Over supper Jane talked non-stop. Sarah laughed at the stories about Perry, and listened eagerly to anything about Gil. 'What's that on your left hand?' she asked.

Jane showed her the plastic ring from the funfair, and Sarah smiled. 'It's perfect,' she said. 'What now?'

'I don't know. The future is so full of problems, but when I'm with Gil I can't seem to remember them,' Jane confessed.

'Then don't think about it. Trust Gil, and everything will come right.'

It was an effort to return to work and wrap herself again in the sedate atmosphere that had once suited her so well. She felt like a different person, and she knew that in the essentials that was what she was. She'd been to the heavens and talked with the stars, and nothing would ever be the same again.

Gil called every day, and she consoled herself with the love in his voice, but he didn't mention a definite date for his return, and gradually a slight shadow crept over her heart.

The photographs she'd taken on the trip had turned out well, and now they had to console her for his absence. There was Gil, his wicked smile stirring her heart; there were the two of them, herself leaning back against him, he looking down at her with an expression of tenderness. There was Perry, beaming into the camera. He too had become part of her life.

One morning, when she'd been back a week, Jane arrived at work to find a note on her desk from her secretary.

'Mr Morgan will be here to see you at 11 a.m.'

Jane drew a slow breath. Henry Morgan was the supercritical boss from head office who'd always made her feel nervous. He'd allowed her to take the four weeks, but his sudden descent on her was an ominous sign.

It's the holiday, she thought. Four whole weeks, when I was so recently appointed. I shouldn't have done it.

But although her head argued sensibly her heart remembered the blissful time she'd spent with Gil and couldn't regret a moment of it.

At eleven o'clock precisely Henry Morgan appeared in her office. He was a man in his mid-fifties with a lean, ascetic face that frequently wore a look of chill superiority. But today, to Jane's amazement, he was actually smiling.

'Welcome back, Miss Landers. Or should I say congratulations?'

'Congratulations, Mr Morgan?'

'You've certainly been hiding your light under a bushel. Your methods may be unconventional, but even an old established bank must move with the times if it's to maximise profits. The very skilful way you've been working to land a big fish has been watched from head office with admiration.'

'Mr Morgan, I really don't know what you're talking about. What "big fish"?'

'I'm talking about Dane & Son. You're not going to say you've never heard of it?'

'Of course not. It's one of the biggest stockbroking firms in London—but what does it have to do with me?'

'You ask that when you've just spent a month with the junior partner?'

'I beg your pardon?'

'Gilbert Dane, the "son" of Dane & Son, and the firm's junior partner.'

'But I don't know any Gilbert Dane. I've spent the last month with Gil Wakeham—'

'Wakeham was the maiden name of Gilbert Dane's mother. Has he been using her name? That's interesting. I understand that he has slightly eccentric ideas.'

'There must be some mistake,' Jane said firmly. 'There's no reason to suppose that they're the same man.' But even as she spoke certain memories returned to make her uneasy: Gil's unwillingness to discuss his past or his family, his astute financial knowledge that sat so oddly with the rest of him, Kenneth's insistence that Gil Wakeham didn't exist. And the loan from a stockbroker called Dane. Oh, it couldn't be true! Could it?

'Are you saying you really didn't know his real identity?' Mr Morgan asked. 'Come now, that's a little hard to believe.'

'There are a lot of things about this that are hard to believe,' Jane said grimly.

'I see what it is. He's asked you to preserve his anonymity. Let's leave it that you haven't admitted anything. But the secret can't be kept indefinitely. Dane & Son are holding a big reception tonight. I want you to attend it with me. If they're thinking of giving Kells some of their business, it might be useful to come out into the open.'

He rummaged in his briefcase. 'I brought his file from the cuttings library at head office,' he explained. 'Study it well before tonight. I'll collect you at seven o'clock.'

He departed, leaving Jane too stunned to speak. After staring at the outside of the file for a few moments she told her secretary to hold all calls and opened it.

And there was his picture, staring out at her from a feature cut from a financial magazine. He was several years younger, his hair was shorter, his clothing conservative, but it was Gil.

Jane read the feature with mounting anger. Gil's background was the same as her own—solid, conventional, rooted in the financial and legal professions. Behind the façade, the man who seemed a clown and an anarchist was sober, respectable, and one of the sharpest dealers in the City.

'You fraud,' she breathed. 'You double-dealing, scheming, twisting fraud. You even have a degree in economics.'

The writer had waxed lyrical about Gilbert Dane's abilities, the brilliance with which he'd modernised an old established firm until it was a feared competitor on the financial scene. Words danced before Jane's eyes. 'Ruthless...predatory...a man to be feared...' This was the real Gil.

She came to another, more personal magazine feature, which described Gil's lifestyle, the luxury flat in London, the expensive tastes. Jane gripped the paper tightly. One thing stood out with shocking clarity. He was in no need of money. The two thousand pounds he'd begged so charmingly had been chicken-feed to him.

But the worst was yet to come. Turning the page, Jane found another picture of him. It had been taken at some social gathering, and showed him in a dinner jacket, laughing with friends, a champagne glass in his hand. Beside him was a young woman in evening dress, her right hand tucked possessively into Gil's arm, her left sporting a very large, flashy ring on the third finger. The caption read:

> Gilbert Dane and his beautiful fiancée, Constance Allbright, daughter of millionaire financier Brian Allbright. The wedding, expected any moment, will unite two of the oldest established City families.

Jane lowered the page, feeling sick with betrayal. Gil was engaged, perhaps married. And he'd played a heartless, cynical game with her. Maybe he'd even been laughing at her all along.

Why? her mind cried. *Why?* But did it really matter why? She'd been the victim of as cruel a trick as any man could devise, and as the first shock passed she was filled with fury. She began to look forward to the evening ahead.

She was ready at seven o'clock, elegantly dressed in a close-fitting black cocktail dress that enhanced her blonde hair and fair skin. Over it she wore a black velvet evening coat. Small diamonds flashed in her ears. She'd made up with great care to be a shade more glamorous than her normal self, and the effect was exactly what she wanted. There was no trace now of the urchin of the last month.

Henry Morgan looked her over with satisfaction, grunted to indicate that she was a credit to the bank, and showed her to his chauffeur-driven Rolls. During the hour-long drive he discussed the benefits that Kells would enjoy from an association with Dane & Son, and Jane tried to concentrate.

The reception was held at a luxurious hotel in the heart of London. The large room was already crowded when they arrived. Gilt chandeliers hung from the ceiling and mirrors lined the walls, throwing back the reflections of hundreds of well-dressed people, laughing, chattering and drinking. They all looked cheerful and confident, and to Jane it felt strange to be here among them when her heart was breaking. But she put her head up, fixed a smile on her face, and responded to introductions as though she hadn't a care in the world.

And then, suddenly, the crowd parted, and she saw Gil. Not the Gil of the past month, the man who'd laughed with her, loved her and made her heart sing, but the other Gil, the one in the picture, wearing a dinner jacket and bow-tie, his hair tidy. He was listening to an elderly man apparently telling a joke, smiling politely.

Beside him was Constance Allbright. She had a loud laugh, a loud voice, and a way of waving her arms about that made people clutch their drinks to their chests. She wore a long, fussy dress of green satin that, however unbecoming, looked as if it had cost a lot of money. Her jewels, too, spoke of wealth. Emeralds adorned her neck, ears and wrists. But the jewel that riveted Jane's attention was the engagement ring on her left hand.

Jane waited without moving, her eyes fixed on Gil. At last her steady gaze seemed to pierce his consciousness. He turned his head, and saw her. For a long moment they regarded each other, while some of the colour drained out of his face. She saw him close his eyes for a moment, as if in horror.

He moved towards her. 'Jane...'

'Good evening, Mr Dane,' she said coolly. 'Such a delightful reception, isn't it? A great success. But then, I understand that everything Dane & Son touches is successful.'

'Jane, please,' he said in a low, hurried voice. 'Don't judge me without listening to me.'

'But I've done nothing but listen to you for the last month, Mr Dane.'

'Don't call me that,' he begged.

'Isn't it your name? I was told that it was—although not by you.'

'To you I'm Gil,' he said urgently. 'Gil Wakeham. We have to find a quiet place and talk. I didn't want you to find out like this.'

'You didn't want me to find out at all,' she said bitterly.

'That's not true. I meant to tell you. I wanted complete honesty between us but—'

'You amaze me, Mr Dane,' she interrupted him. 'Your actions this last month didn't suggest a man who wanted complete honesty.'

'I know that, and I'm sorry. I never meant to deceive you. It got out of hand. Please give me a chance to explain.'

'There's no way you can explain it away,' she said angrily. 'And you insult me by thinking I'd be fooled a second time.' She saw Constance closing in on them, and said brightly, 'You must introduce me to your delightful fiancée. Or is it your wife now? I'm afraid I'm rather out of touch.'

'No, we're not married yet,' Constance said with a giggle.

'But I'm sure you will be very soon,' Jane said. 'Any man who could buy such a magnificent engagement ring must be very devoted.'

'Isn't it beautiful?' Constance said with another giggle. 'Darling Gilbert said that only the best was good enough for me. I'm Connie Allbright.' She gave Jane a bland look. 'Who are you?'

'My name is Jane Landers. I'm the manager of a small branch of Kells Bank.'

'Oh, yes, they really do have women bank managers these days, don't they?' Connie said, as though Jane were a kind of freak. 'Gil told me he'd met a few funny ones, didn't you, darling?'

'No, I didn't,' Gil said firmly. 'You must have misunderstood me.'

'Nonsense. You and I have a perfect understanding. We're always saying so.'

Gil's face was tight with anger. 'Connie—'

'Please don't stop Miss Allbright saying anything she wants to,' Jane said. 'I'm finding it so interesting.' Her eyes met Gil's. 'And instructive.'

She heard him draw a sharp breath, but before he could speak a tall man appeared at his elbow and said, 'Gil, m'boy—'

They were strikingly alike and Jane wasn't surprised when Gil introduced him as his father. They talked polite nothings for a few minutes, then Dane senior drew his son away to talk to someone, and Jane was left with Connie.

'I'm fascinated to meet you, Miss Allbright,' Jane said. 'I saw your photograph in a magazine.'

'Which one? Oh, well, it doesn't matter. I lose track. They all want to know the same things, don't they? Darling Gil simply hates being photographed, but I say one has one's social duty. Don't you think?'

'Without a doubt,' Jane responded. 'I dare say he listens to you.'

'Oh, well, of course we grew up together. I probably know him better than anyone else in the world, so I can say things he wouldn't take from anyone else.'

'I'm sure you can,' Jane said politely.

'Like recently I teased him about being born with a silver spoon in his mouth. Gil has expensive tastes, but he's never been short of money to cater for them. I asked him how he'd manage if he had to fend for himself.

'So what do you think the darling did? He set out to prove to me that he could succeed in business on his own, without making any use of his family's money. Wasn't that charming of him—like a knight of old proving himself to his lady?'

'Charming,' Jane said in a colourless voice.

'He's been driving round the country in some ghastly old van giving firework displays. Isn't that funny?'

'Hilarious,' Jane agreed. 'It must have warmed your heart to know that he'd go to such lengths for you.'

'Oh, it did. You'd never think it to look at him, but under that formal exterior my Gil is a real old-fashioned romantic at heart.'

Jane nodded. 'Yes, I can believe he's quite different from the way he seems.'

'Of course I telephoned him along the way, to encourage him.'

'So I imagined,' Jane murmured.

'He loved that. He said it meant the world to him to know that he still had his lady's favour. Wasn't that a sweet thing for him to say?'

'Perfectly adorable,' Jane agreed.

She seemed to be answering from the top of her brain, while underneath she seethed with misery and anger. Luckily Henry Morgan was on the other side of the room, deep in conversation. He'd praised Jane's talents in landing 'a big fish'. She wondered what he would say if he knew how completely she'd been taken for a fool by a heartless schemer.

Connie was unstoppable now. 'He's so sentimental,' she burbled on, 'he even insisted on taking my dog.'

'Your dog?'

'Pericles. Gil gave him to me as an engagement present. We chose him together when he was a puppy, but when Gil said he was going out into the world to prove himself I let Pericles go with him—to remind him of me.'

Jane felt she would go mad if she had to listen to any more. It was a relief when Henry Morgan beckoned her over to introduce her to someone.

Somehow she got through the rest of the evening. Gil didn't approach her again. She saw him once or twice, always with Connie hanging on his arm. And when it was time to go, and she was getting into Morgan's car, she saw Gilbert Dane and Connie coming through the car park. She was hanging onto his arm and giggling. His face was dark, and Jane guessed he was furious at having his deception exposed. He was probably wondering if Jane had told Connie enough to put his profitable marriage in doubt.

Connie and Gilbert Dane stopped beside a top-of-the-range sports car that would have supported Gil Wakeham for a year. He opened the door and she got into the passenger seat. As Jane watched, with a little pain in her heart, he got in beside her and drove away.

As they went home Mr Morgan said, 'Well done, Miss Landers.'

'I beg your pardon?'

'Dane & Son are putting a lot of business our way. Several local industries have attracted their attention as good investment possibilities.'

'That's excellent, but I'm sure it needn't involve me.'

'You sound as though you don't want to be involved.'

'There's a much larger branch of Kells in Wellhampton. Dane & Son will naturally go to them.'

'Normally, yes. But they have a lot of clout. If they want to come to you, that's what they'll do. Besides, I should like to see you get credit for your splendid work. I won't deny that I had my doubts about your youth when you were first appointed. But you've proved me wrong. Well done. I think after tonight we can say that you're in the fast track, and your future's looking rosy. Very rosy indeed.'

CHAPTER ELEVEN

THE phone on Jane's desk rang and she snatched it up. 'Yes?' she enquired crisply.

'It's him again,' her secretary said.

'Then why are you telling me? I thought I'd made it plain that I don't want to take Mr Dane's calls.'

'I've explained that you won't talk to him, but he won't give up.'

'I'm aware of that,' Jane said, tight-lipped.

'Every half-hour for the last two days. I wish an attractive man would pursue me like that.'

'You don't know what you're talking about. Mr Dane is *not* an attractive man. He's a fraud and a cheat.'

'Well, he's sent you a message.'

'I don't wish to receive it.'

'He says Perry is pining for you.'

Jane drew an angry breath. 'That has to be the most unscrupulous, outrageous—words fail me. Are there no depths to which he won't sink?'

'What shall I tell him?'

'Tell him I don't wish to speak to him.'

'What about Perry?'

'Perry is as big a fraud as his master,' Jane said, and replaced the receiver firmly.

She was half afraid Gil would call back at once, as he had sometimes done over the last two days, but to her relief the phone remained silent.

She had drawn a line under Gil, determined to put him out of her life. What had happened between them was an aberration—one that, with her usual efficiency, she would soon put right.

Sarah, of course, disagreed with her. 'You shouldn't judge poor Gil without giving him a chance to explain,' she'd insisted when Jane had told her what had happened.

'He isn't "poor Gil". He deceived me.'

'There may be some innocent explanation. You won't know if you don't talk to him.'

'Sarah, what's come over you? At one time you'd have been the first to condemn him.'

'At one time I made a lot of very glib judgements. I've grown wiser now, and it's time you did the same.'

'Don't worry about me,' Jane said. 'I'm wiser, I promise you.'

For two days there were no more calls. Jane told herself that she was glad Gil had finally seen sense. There was an ache in her heart, but she refused to face that.

Then Henry Morgan telephoned again.

'I've just come off the line from a long talk with Alex Dane, the senior partner. He wants to set up an early meeting. I've told him you're free at three o'clock this afternoon.'

'Certainly. Do you want me to come in to head office?'

'No, he feels that Wellhampton is the proper place to talk, and I agree with him. I thought of joining you, but I'm sure you can manage without me. Head office is extremely pleased with you.'

Jane hung up with mixed feelings. She'd tried to put a distance between herself and Gil, and now it seemed she had to deal with his father. She reminded herself that head office was pleased with her. If she made a success of this there was nowhere she couldn't climb.

Yet somehow that thought didn't thrill her as once it would have done.

At five minutes to three her desk was clear and she was ready. When her secretary announced, 'Mr Dane,' she faced the door with her head up and a smile of welcome fixed onto her face.

But the smile faded as Mr Dane appeared in the doorway. *'You!'* she exclaimed. 'How dare you come here?'

'But I have an appointment,' Gil said. 'For three o'clock.'

'That was supposed to be Alex Dane,' she said furiously.

'My father leaves this kind of thing to me. Mostly, anyway. I asked him to deal with your head office because—well, just because.'

'Because you knew I wouldn't agree to this meeting if I knew it was you,' she said. 'I want you to leave, right now.'

'I can't. We have business to transact. I'm an official representative of Dane & Son. What would your bosses say if you threw me out?'

'My bosses can go and—jump in the lake,' Jane said distractedly.

'You don't mean that. You have a brilliant career to think of,' he reminded her.

Jane faced him, her eyes smouldering. Gil was dressed in a formal suit, with a white shirt and conservative tie. He looked every inch the stockbroker. Yet there was still a gleam in his eyes that sent a tremor through her. She tried to stop it happening, tried to be sensible. Then she remembered how he'd deceived her, and suddenly it was easy to be sensible.

'Very well, Mr Dane, let's get down to business,' she said coolly. 'May I offer you some coffee?'

'Jane, please don't talk like that. I did this because I had to. You must let me talk to you—explain—'

'Explain? Do you think anything can explain away lying to me and betraying your fiancée?'

'Connie is not my fiancée,' Gil said flatly. 'She had no right to give you that impression.'

'Oh, please! I didn't imagine that huge ring, did I?'

'No, but—'

'And you did buy it for her?'

'Will you let me get a word in edgeways? Connie's family and mine have been friends for years and our parents wanted us to get married. I refused, because I wasn't in love with her, but in a weak moment I gave in. My mother was seriously ill and I thought it would please her. I took Connie to buy a ring and she chose the most expensive one in the shop. She's a lady who likes the biggest and best of everything.

'I don't know what would have happened if I'd married her. We wouldn't have been happy, I do know that. Luckily my mother recovered, realised how I felt, and advised me not to go through with it.

'Connie was understanding. I was so grateful to her for being nice about it that I let her keep the ring. That's how she comes to have it. And don't think she's been heartbroken for me, because all this was a year ago, and she's been engaged to someone else since. When that ended she took to wearing my ring again, and dropping hints. She's not in love with me, any more than I am with her. She's just decided that I'm better than nothing. I don't like it, but I can't very easily demand the ring back after all this time.'

'And Perry? Wasn't he hers?'

'Oh, yes,' Gil said grimly. 'Perry. The dog she insisted on having because he was such a sweet little puppy. I warned her that the little puppy would grow into an animal who needed a lot of exercise, but she wouldn't listen. In the end she discovered I was right and wanted to have him put down. I couldn't let her do that. So I took him back.'

'And what about the rest?' Jane asked, eyeing him steadily. 'She told me how she urged you to prove yourself in your own business, and telephoned you along the way to show that you still had your "lady's favour".'

'It's true that Connie taunted me with having things easy because of my background, but I took up the idea because I was thrilled at the thought of striking out on my own. I wasn't trying to prove myself to her.' He looked at Jane, aware that somehow he was failing to get through to her. There was no softening in her face.

'My background's the same as yours,' he said. 'My relatives are solid professionals—bankers, lawyers, stockbrokers—and that's just the women! I grew up knowing there was a place for me in the family firm. All I had to do was pass the exams. It was all so easy. Too easy. Then a few months ago Connie said, "A real man makes his own place in the world." I knew she was only trying to make me jealous of a self-made man she'd started dating, but something inside me said, *Yes!*

'I took an extended leave and cut myself off from my background as far as possible. I called myself Wakeham because I didn't want to capitalise on the family name. I bought an old caravan and started from scratch. The only concession I made to the past was to persuade Gil Wakeham to ask Gilbert Danc for a loan.'

The old smile appeared faintly on Gil's face as he tried to draw her into one of his jokes. 'Gil Wakeham didn't want to. In fact Gilbert Dane didn't want to either. He regards Gil as you did that first day: as a dodgy character. But Gil talked him round.'

'Yes, you told me, the day I saw your notebook.'

'That's right. Mr Dane made Gil a loan, but at a tough rate of interest. No favours. Gil paid it all back, although sometimes a bit erratically. Once he couldn't make a payment in time, and they had a difficult scene. Gil made some very frank comments about Mr Dane's shortcomings, so when he needed another loan he didn't feel he could return to that source.'

Gil finished with a grimace as he saw that Jane hadn't thawed under his humour.

'Jane, darling, I love you. Every word I've said is the truth. I never set out to deceive you. In the beginning, you were just a bank manager. But I soon fell in love with you, and I dared to hope you loved me. Or rather, that you loved Gil Wakeham. It was too late to tell you the truth then. I kept meaning to, and chickening out in case I lost you.

'The other night I took Connie home and had it out with her. I made her tell me everything she'd said, and I was horrified. I see how she made it look, but I swear there's nothing between Connie and me. I told her straight that she could forget any idea of marriage because I love you.'

'You don't see it, do you?' she asked softly. 'You think this is just about Connie, and you simply don't see what you've done. You deceived me.'

'But I've explained that Connie and I—'

'I don't mean her,' she interrupted. 'I mean all that stuff about the open road, and never knowing what tomorrow would bring: being a free spirit who only cared about the beauty in the sky and never mind about material things. And it was all a lie, because actually you're a rich man who can afford all the material things he wants. The open road was fine as long as you could go home to a penthouse suite whenever it suited you. You—you *stockbroker*!' She uttered the last word with loathing.

Gil grew pale. 'It was only a few weeks ago that a stockbroker was a marvellous person in your eyes.'

'But you taught me differently,' she cried. 'And it was just a game to you.'

'It's more than that—'

'Oh, really! You say you cut yourself off from your background, but you were at that function the other evening, weren't you?'

'I can't cut myself off completely, for my father's sake.'

'How convenient!' she scoffed. 'It's all play-acting, nothing more. And when you tire of it you'll go back to your real life, won't you, Mr Dane?'

He winced. 'I wish you wouldn't call me that. I'm Gil Wakeham.'

'Gil Wakeham doesn't exist,' she cried. 'He's just a pretend man living a pretend life. Well, I'm tired of being part of your pretence.' She drew a painful breath. 'It's over.'

He stared at her. 'What do you mean—over?'

'The joke's over. The game's over. I loaned you two thousand pounds because I thought you needed it.'

'But I do—'

'Nonsense! Go back to Gilbert Dane.'

'I can't. He won't have anything more to do with me.'

'Stop talking as if you were two people.'

'But that's just it. We are. There's something I haven't told you, and it's the most difficult part. It wasn't just about proving my ability to make a living on my own.

I took a good hard look at myself and didn't like what I saw.

'Gilbert Dane was a money-making machine with an eye to the main chance and no thought for anything else. He never had the time of day for people because he couldn't raise his eyes from the figures long enough. I didn't want to be him any more. I knew there was another side to me, but I'd never given it a chance to develop.

'That other side is Gil Wakeham. At first it felt strange to be him, but then he began to take over and feel natural. He *is* natural. He's who I want to be. And then I met you, and loved you. And you loved me. At least, you loved Gil Wakeham, and I want to go on being the man you loved. But I need you to help me. Without you I may go back to being Gilbert Dane again, and I don't want to do that. Don't send me back to him, Jane, I beg you.'

But she stopped her ears and turned away. 'It's all words,' she said. 'You're clever with words. You should have told me the truth before.'

'I was afraid to, afraid of spoiling what we had, when it was so perfect.'

'It's too late—'

'It mustn't be too late,' he said passionately. 'Help me, Jane. Don't ask me to repay you now, because if I have to use Dane money I've failed. I *must* get Joe Stebbins's contract.'

'Then let's hope you get it,' Jane said crisply.

'How can I, without your help? We've arranged the big displays so that they need two of us to work them.'

'Get Tommy. He'll be thrilled.'

'Tommy's away on a Youth Training Scheme on a sailing ship in the Channel. I can't reach him. Besides, I want you. We worked this show out together. Please,

Jane; it means so much to me. I'm doing another show in Wellhampton next week, and Stebbins is going to be there. Give me a little time, just long enough to do that display for him. Then I can get an advance and repay you from my own work.'

'Very well,' she said at last. 'Two weeks.'

'And you'll help me with the display?'

'Oh, no. I'm setting off no more fireworks.'

'At least come and look at it. There's a message in there that's just for you.'

'Can't you understand that those days are over?' she cried. 'You fooled me once, but not a second time.'

Gil stood looking at her steadily. There was something in his face that broke her heart, but she refused to yield. After a moment she pulled herself together.

'Are you ready to discuss business now?' she asked.

He seemed to come out of a dream. 'Very well,' he said quietly. 'I have some papers here for you to look at. They contain proposals which my firm thinks...'

She forced herself to concentrate for the next two hours. She was functioning on automatic, but her well-trained brain digested the figures and produced the right responses. Gil was clearly an expert, also with a mind that could hold facts and figures and juggle them with ease. In fact he was exactly what she would once have called 'my kind of man'. But not any more, she thought bitterly. Not any more.

When the time was up he looked at her in concern and said gently, 'You look ill. My poor darling, forgive me. I didn't mean to—'

'My health is perfect, thank you,' Jane checked him. 'I'll be in touch with you about these proposals in a couple of days.'

After a moment he said, 'Thank you, Miss Landers. I shall report to my father that he has every reason to be pleased with his decision to use Kells. I'll make sure your head office knows too.'

'Don't do me any favours,' Jane said fiercely.

'I'm not. You're an excellent bank manager, Jane. You should go a long way. I wish you every success in your career.'

Then he was gone, and there was no need any longer to fight back the tears.

Three evenings later, as Jane went through her front door she heard the sound of voices. She went in quickly, smiling with pleasure.

'Tony,' she cried, delighted at the sight of her favourite brother. He jumped up and gave her a vigorous hug. He was twenty-eight, with a baby face and laughing eyes. But they hadn't laughed so often since he'd 'seen sense' and given up the stage, Jane realised.

When they'd exclaimed over each other and Sarah had brought in some tea, Jane asked, 'How's Delia?' Delia was the boss's daughter in the bank where Tony worked, and the family was hourly expecting an announcement.

'She's fine,' Tony said cautiously.

'But?'

'Well, we were going to get engaged, and then Jim, my agent, called. At least, he isn't my agent any more, since I left acting. But he reckoned there was a job I was just right for, and he called me on the off chance.'

'You mean an acting job?' Jane asked.

'That's right. A new television police series. They need someone for the hero's sidekick. With my funny face Jim reckons I'd be perfect. I've auditioned, and the job's mine if I want it, but it would mean leaving the bank, and it might only be for twelve episodes. Then—' He shrugged eloquently.

'But it's your chance,' Jane breathed. 'You've been longing for this.'

'If only it had come sooner,' Tony sighed. 'I used to dream of being a big star—Hamlet, Romeo, all that. Well, it's not going to happen, not with my face. But Jim reckons if I do this series I'll get known. Then I could have a good career as a character actor. "Never in lights, but always in work" is how he put it.'

'What does Delia say?'

He sighed. 'Delia hit the roof when I did the audition. She says her father would be very disappointed at my lack of responsibility. I just don't know what to do.'

'Oh, yes, you do,' Sarah said robustly. 'You know exactly what's the right thing to do. Take that job, and tell Delia's father to take a running jump. And tell her to take one too if she won't stand by you. If she doesn't love you enough for that, you're better off without her.'

Tony stared at his grandmother, with his mouth open. 'That was *you* talking, wasn't it?' he asked, bewildered.

'Sarah's changed,' Jane said. 'Haven't you heard?'

'Something, yes. Father—well, you know he's not very tactful and he said—'

'He said the silly old woman had gone off her rocker,' Sarah supplied calmly. 'I can just hear him. He always was the stuffiest of my sons. But you're not like him, thank goodness. You're like me. I wanted to go on the stage once. I gave up my chance, and ever since then I've wondered what would have happened if—'

Sarah stopped suddenly, and drew a breath. Jane knew she was remembering not just the stage, but also the man she'd once loved. She put her hand over Sarah's, and felt her grandmother squeeze it gratefully.

'Whatever you do,' Sarah went on, 'don't spend your life wondering what would have happened.' She looked at Jane as she spoke. 'Follow your heart. Do what it tells you. And ignore anyone who says anything different.'

'I'll do it,' Tony said with sudden resolution.

'Call Jim from here,' Sarah said. 'Make it definite.'

Tony made the call at once, and the two women watched him in delight. It was good to see someone happy, Jane thought. Sarah was beaming, and Jane guessed there was a special satisfaction for her in helping Tony avoid her own mistake.

At last Tony came off the phone and gave a whoop of delight. 'Jim says I've got to get round there quick. Thanks, both of you. In five years' time, when I'm giving press interviews, I'll tell the world I owe it all to you. *Yippee!*'

He kissed them both quickly and vanished. Jane and Sarah looked at each other and smiled.

As Jane made the supper she asked, 'Did you go out today?' She was half expecting a negative reply. It seemed to her that Sarah went out less these days.

But Sarah said, 'Oh, yes. I had lunch with a charming young man. We had a very interesting talk.'

Jane looked at her for a moment in silence. 'Gil, I suppose?' she said at last. 'How could you?'

'Because I like him, and because I think you're being very hard on him. Perhaps he should have told you the truth earlier, but I can see why he'd have found it difficult.

'Don't you remember that first evening you brought him to meet me, and he played his part so badly? I said it was clear he wasn't used to acting a role. It's true. He wasn't acting when he was with you. He was being something different.

'I think he's one of the most honest people I've ever met, and one of the bravest. To do what he did—take a hard look at himself, and decide he didn't like himself, and was going to change—that took a lot of strength.

'Jane, dear, wasn't it the same with you? Didn't you change when you were with him, find a new person inside yourself, a *happier* person? Are you going to throw it away?'

'I can't help it,' she said huskily. 'There's something inside me that just can't give in about this. Please, Sarah, don't say any more. Don't—don't—'

'Darling, I didn't mean to upset you. It's just that I want you to be happy, and there's so little time left. There, don't cry. Come to your gran. Don't cry—don't cry...'

CHAPTER TWELVE

FOUR days till Gil's show: three days, two, one. Jane tried not to notice the passing of time, but a part of her mind persisted in pointing it out. It was a struggle to do everything now. A struggle to work, a struggle to sleep, a struggle not to cry. But, as she'd said to Sarah, there was something in her that couldn't yield. What she'd thought was reality had been only a play, and now the curtain had come down.

The only bright spot was a call from Tony to say he'd signed his contract. 'Delia was wonderful about it,' he said. 'We're getting married at once so that we can have a honeymoon before I start shooting.'

Sarah seemed more tired suddenly. She didn't go out so much and sometimes Jane caught her looking sad. When the evening came, Sarah kept looking at the clock.

'I know what day it is,' Jane said. 'I haven't forgotten.'

'Then shouldn't you be there?' Sarah asked gently.

'No, it's the last place I should be.'

'But it means so much to him,' Sarah pleaded. 'He needs your help with the display so that he can get this contract.'

'You're forgetting that he's a stockbroker. You talk as though the fireworks business is vital to him, but it isn't.'

'Of course it is!' Sarah said, almost angrily. 'He's trying to prove himself as a man, and he enlisted your help. Not Connie's. Yours. That's a pretty high compliment. He stripped the trappings away and showed you what he really was. Are you going to throw it all back at him, tell him he's not good enough?'

'Perhaps we never really had a chance,' Jane said sadly. 'We're too different.'

'Too much alike, you mean. He told me that without you he's afraid of going back to being Gilbert Dane. Without him, perhaps *you* should be afraid of going back to being Miss Landers, bank manager, and nothing else.'

Nine o'clock came and went. Jane knew what Gil would be doing now: making the final adjustments, checking everything twice. He would be nervous, as a great artist always was before a major performance, but he would hide it beneath a smile.

She shut her mind off. She wouldn't let her thoughts dwell on Gil. That way lay weakness. But Sarah's words haunted her. 'Miss Landers, bank manager, and nothing else.'

Sarah went to bed early, leaving Jane working on a report. She made herself some tea, and discovered she was running low on milk. There was just time to slip down to the corner shop that stayed open late. She snatched up her purse and opened the front door.

But there she stopped, thunderstruck by what she found outside.

'Andrew!' she gasped. 'What are you doing here?'

The old man looked at her from behind the biggest bouquet of red roses that Jane had ever seen. His face, for the first time ever, was sheepish.

'I've been here half an hour,' he confessed. 'I kept getting ready to knock and losing my nerve.'

'Come in. Sarah's gone to bed, but I'll call her.'

'No, don't do that. I'm not quite ready. Could we talk first?'

Jane settled him on the sofa and laid the roses carefully aside. They told, more eloquently than words, why he'd come here.

'How is she?' Andrew asked with painful eagerness.

'Coping,' Jane said. 'But not so well recently.'

'When we've talked on the phone she's always spoken as though she's living it up.'

'She was, at first. But I think it's begun to pall and she's not very happy.' Jane added guiltily, 'But don't tell her I told you that.'

'No, she's a very difficult woman, your grandmother.'

'Just her?' Jane asked lightly.

He gave another sheepish grin, but didn't answer.

'How are you coping?' Jane asked. 'Entertained any young women recently?'

'Young women!' he said in accents of scorn. 'What do they know, any of them? Oh, I messed about for the first couple of weeks—made a complete fool of myself probably—but I soon got fed up.' He gave an awkward laugh. 'I miss her, you know, Jane. Miss her like the very devil.'

'You should have come here before,' Jane said gently.

'How could I when she made it so obvious she didn't want me?' Andrew gave a heavy sigh. 'It's always been the way.'

'What has?'

'She's never wanted me, not really. It was always that other fellow. The actor she was in love with.'

Jane stared. 'I thought you didn't know about him.'

'Of course I knew. When I was courting her, I called at her parents' house one evening. She was out, but she got home soon. I saw her come through the garden gate with this fellow. He was good-looking, sure of himself, everything I wasn't. They got as far as the front door, but she didn't come in. There was just a long silence, and I knew she was kissing him. I'd always thought heartbreak was just fancy talk, but it wasn't. It was what I felt while I knew she was out there in his arms.

'Then she came in. She didn't see me watching her. She was holding a single red rose, and from the way she kissed it I could tell he'd given it to her. She loved him, not me.

'I knew I should walk out, but I couldn't. I loved her so much. She was such a pretty little thing, with big, innocent eyes—I'd have done anything for her.

'She married me, but only because she couldn't have the other chap. I tried to tell myself that she'd grow to love me, but one day—' He checked himself, as though the memory was too painful for words.

'One day—what?' Jane asked. All her senses were alert. Out of the corner of her eye she could see that the door to Sarah's room had opened a little.

'It was her birthday,' Andrew recalled. 'I planned a big party for her, and at the end of the evening I was going to give her the biggest bouquet of red roses you ever saw. It was a wonderful evening. I thought everything was going to be all right at last. But then someone mentioned his name casually, and there was such a look on her face—and I knew she still loved him. I went and threw the roses away.'

'And you've never given her roses, all these years?' Jane asked, torn with pity for a man she'd always thought of as stolid and unimaginative.

'There was no point,' Andrew said. 'I knew I'd only ever be second-best.'

There was a sound behind him, half-gasp, half-sob. He turned quickly to see Sarah, tears running down her face. Wordlessly she held open her arms and her husband went into them.

'Darling Andrew, you're not second-best,' she said in a muffled voice. 'You're not, you're *not*.'

'I always hoped you'd turn to me—all these years—'

'I didn't know you knew— Oh, what a fool I've been.' Sarah clasped him more tightly than ever.

Jane backed quietly out of the room. She wasn't needed now. She took the moment to run down for the milk, and when she returned the two old people were sitting on the sofa, holding hands. At some point Sarah had unwrapped her bouquet, and roses lay everywhere, covering her with brilliant crimson, the colour of love.

'Is everything all right?' Jane asked, smiling.

'Everything's wonderful,' Sarah said with a misty smile. 'As wonderful as can be.' She touched her husband's face gently. 'I made the right decision all those years ago. I know it now. My darling, your roses mean more to me than anyone else's ever could.' She looked at Jane. 'You need a man who can give you both sides—the freedom and the safety. You could have that, but you're throwing it away. Hurry, before it's too late.'

Suddenly Jane was afraid. As though coloured lights had slid away from her eyes she saw clearly what pride and anger had almost made her do. Gil had pleaded for her to understand and help him achieve his dream. But she'd spurned him. She looked at her watch. It was half-past nine. There wasn't much time...

'Drive safely,' Sarah called as Jane turned to the door. The moment it had closed behind her the two old people were in each other's arms again.

Jane tried to heed the warning, but what she wanted to do was step on the accelerator. She forced herself to stay calm until the grounds came into sight. As she parked she could hear the announcement over the loud-speaker, saying that the fireworks were about to start. Crowds were drifting to the far end of the grounds. Jane began to run.

Heedless of where she was going, she collided with Joe Stebbins. 'I thought you weren't coming,' he said. 'Pity you couldn't get here before. Gil's had a heck of a time setting it all up by himself.'

'Where is he?' Jane asked frantically.

'Making some last-minute adjustments over there.'

Jane followed his pointing arm and saw Gil climbing up the scaffolding. *'Gil!'* she cried. 'Gil—I love you.'

He twisted to look over his shoulder. His face lit up with joy and he instinctively reached out a hand to her. Then it happened. His other hand wasn't secure. He began to slip, struggled desperately to hold on, and the next moment was plunging to earth. Jane screamed as she saw him hit the ground with a sickening thud.

She rushed over to where he was lying. His face was contorted with pain and he was gasping. She reached out her hands, then snatched them back, fearful of hurting him more.

'Darling,' she cried, 'I'm so sorry. I should have come before.'

Gil managed to smile through his pain. 'Never mind. You're here now. Kiss me.'

She leaned down and gathered him gently in her arms. With his good hand he reached up to slide his fingers behind her head.

'That was a nasty crack,' Joe Stebbins said, coming up to them. 'Hear it a mile away. Sounded like a broken bone.'

'Yes, I think it's my collar bone,' Gil gasped painfully.

'There's a medical team on the far side of the field,' Joe said. 'I'll fetch them.'

'No!' Gil cried fiercely. 'Not yet. Not till I've given the show.'

'You can't give a show in your state,' Joe protested.

'Are you going to give me the contract without it?' Gil demanded.

'Well, no; I need to see you do something bigger than I saw last time. But perhaps next year—'

'Next year will be too late,' Gil said frantically. 'It's now or never.'

'Darling, it doesn't matter,' Jane pleaded.

'It does,' he insisted. 'Don't you understand why it matters?'

In a burst of light like the explosion of a rocket, everything became blindingly clear to her. Gil's pride and his dream were at stake, and only her love could save them.

'All right, then,' she said. 'We'll do it together. You tell me how it's arranged, and I'll set it off.'

She could feel him relax in her arms as he raised his glowing face to hers. 'Help me up,' he said painfully.

He showed her the bank of switches. 'That one first, to set off the shooting stars. The next one is noise rockets, then whistling candles...'

Jane concentrated, trying to take it all in, and very quickly she found it was coming naturally. The weeks of working with Gil had made her familiar with his mind, and she found she could anticipate almost every move.

'Then the ones at the back,' she said. 'Display rockets, thunder candles, shells...'

'That's it,' he said with relief. 'You've got it.' He fell into a chair Joe had found for him.

There was a murmur as the crowd approached. 'Kiss me for luck,' she said.

They kissed each other, then it was time to start. Gil started the music. Jane touched the first switch and colours zoomed overhead.

It was glorious, like being the conductor of a huge orchestra. Switch after switch, everything responding exactly to her command, the sky alight with beauty. And they'd done it together. Basically this was the show she and Gil had planned, and his genius had made it work.

He'd switched on a powerful torch, using the beam to guide her from one step to the next. Sometimes she caught his eye. He was smiling encouragement through his pain, and she knew he was thinking the same as herself. They were a fantastic team, and they always would be.

Not much more to go: just the set piece.

'Where's the switch?' she cried. 'Shine the torch.'

But instead Gil hoisted himself painfully to his feet. 'I'll do it,' he said unsteadily. 'I want you to watch from the front.'

Jane suppressed her instinctive protest. There was a sense of purpose about him that told her this was something that mattered to him more than pain. So she backed away, watching anxiously as he made his way to the switches. He threw the last one, and the fireworks on the scaffolding began to crackle. One after another they flamed into life, deep rose-red, forming a petal, then another and another, until the whole perfect picture became clear.

It was a red rose, just as he had once promised her. Jane watched it form with awe and delight, and her heart overflowed with happiness.

As the crowd applauded she ran to him. His brow was damp with strain, but there was a look of triumph in his eyes. 'I promised you,' he gasped. 'That was the message I wanted you to see. It means...'

'I know what it means,' she said. 'Oh, darling, I love you so much.'

'Ready to go now, sir?' A paramedic indicated the waiting ambulance.

'Not yet,' Gil said. 'Where's Joe?'

Joe Stebbins appeared. 'Wonderful!' he said. 'As soon as you're better we'll discuss the contract.'

The ambulance doors shut, enclosing Gil and Jane together. At once his lips were on hers. 'I was so afraid you wouldn't come,' he said. 'But then I told myself that what we had was too special to be lost. I'm sorry about everything I did wrong, sorry that you found out that way...'

'Don't be sorry,' she said passionately. 'I should have understood. You were right. What we have is special. Oh, Gil, I almost let it slip away.'

'I wouldn't have let you,' he said. 'I'd have kept on following you...'

'But if I hadn't come here tonight would it have been the same?'

He shook his head. 'No,' he said. 'I'd have loved you anyway, because I'll always love you. But it wouldn't have been the same. But you did come. You were bound to. Loving each other as we do, it couldn't have been any other way. And now I'll never let you go again.'

'So it's back on the road for us?' she asked.

'No. I have to go back to the firm. I can do that now. Wakeham's Wonderful Fireworks was a success, and that's something I'll always have. And you need to be a bank manager and build on all your hard work.'

'You mean the fireworks are over?' she cried. 'Oh, no, you can't mean that.'

'Of course not. When Tommy comes back I'm going to train him to take my place. He'll do the practical stuff most of the time, but you and I will plan the shows, and you'll run the business side. And sometimes we'll go back on the road, at weekends and holidays.'

'And our honeymoon,' she said eagerly.

'Don't you want a tropical beach?'

She shook her head. 'You, me and Perry,' she said. 'That's my idea of a honeymoon.'

'And mine,' he said contentedly. 'In fact it's my idea of perfection, always.'

She leaned down and gently laid her lips on his. Somewhere in the back of her consciousness a firework began to burn. Not a rocket, or anything dazzling and short-lived, but a slow, glowing candle that would burn for ever.

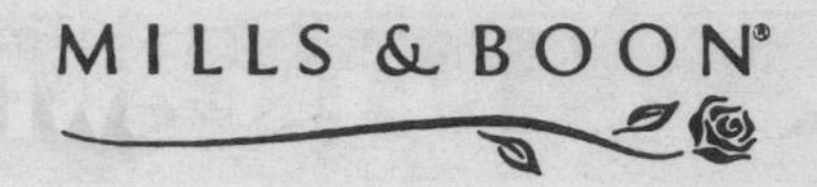

Next Month's Romances

Each month you can choose from a wide variety of romance with Mills & Boon. Below are the new titles to look out for next month in our two new series Presents and Enchanted.

Presents™

THEIR WEDDING DAY	Emma Darcy
THE FINAL PROPOSAL	Robyn Donald
HIS BABY!	Sharon Kendrick
MARRIED FOR REAL	Lindsay Armstrong
MISTLETOE MAN	Kathleen O'Brien
BAD INFLUENCE	Susanne McCarthy
TORN BY DESIRE	Natalie Fox
POWERFUL PERSUASION	Margaret Mayo

Enchanted™

THE VICAR'S DAUGHTER	Betty Neels
BECAUSE OF THE BABY	Debbie Macomber
UNEXPECTED ENGAGEMENT	Jessica Steele
BORROWED WIFE	Patricia Wilson
ANGEL BRIDE	Barbara McMahon
A WIFE FOR CHRISTMAS	Pamela Bauer & Judy Kaye
ALL SHE WANTS FOR CHRISTMAS	Liz Fielding
TROUBLE IN PARADISE	Grace Green

Available from WH Smith, John Menzies, Volume One, Forbuoys, Martins, Woolworths, Tesco, Asda, Safeway and other paperback stockists.